THE TRAIL BLAZERS

THE TRAIL BLAZERS

Tom Curry

CHIVERS

British Library Cataloguing in Publication Data available

This Large Print edition published by AudioGO Ltd, Bath, 2012.
Published by arrangement with Golden West Literary Agency.

U.K. Hardcover   ISBN   978 1 4458 7741 9
U.K. Softcover   ISBN   978 1 4458 7742 6

Printed and bound in Great Britain by
MPG Books Group Limited

THE TRAIL BLAZERS

CHAPTER I:
SAVAGE DEATH

The Texas sun caught the razor summits of the mountains, glowing red as blood. The wilderness seemed calm and at peace. The distant call of birds sounded like a summons to quiet joy and soothing somnolence, and the hovering warmth of the afternoon rested upon the brooding land. It seemed like a place of benign silence where man and Nature could be at peace, yet savage death lurked unseen ready to strike.

The man who topped the rise, peering across to the face of the next ridge, grew taut in his saddle suddenly, and a sharp exclamation left his lips as he saw squatted figures on the steep slope. Engrossed in what they were doing, they failed to observe the glint of the sun along the Winchester rifle barrel which he hastily threw up to firing position.

His hard, evil eyes flashed, a beam of death that presaged the murderous long bullet that tore from the gun's muzzle.

One of the squatting men never finished his task; straightened up again. He took the slug in the ribs, and it tore through to his heart. Like a felled ox he dropped rolling down the hill until sharp rocks snagged his corpse.

It was a time when the West was raw and young, when primitive passions balanced with primitive ways, and at such time, particularly in a place so wild, men moved with infinite caution, guns ever at hand, or they ceased to move at all.

Not for long could a man lower his eyes in the open, from their ever-searching of the wide horizon. Enemies, unseen perhaps, but vengeful, were ever near. Emboldened by the absence of restraint during the epochal struggle of the Civil War, the Apaches, the Comanches, and other fierce tribes rode the deer trails of mighty Texas and through entire wide green spaces of the West.

Scattered settlements slept on hair-trigger when the moon was full, for it was then that raiding parties of feathered painted warriors might be expected to strike. Now, with the war over, the whites were slowly organizing resistance to the red depredations, but the danger was far from past and men still rode knowing that silent death was at their heels.

So it was with the two squatting men on the hillside whose vigilance had grown lax. One had died instantly — without even hearing the wings of the Angel of Death as they brushed by.

The other man, at the crack of the killer's Winchester, acted on the instant, hoping for a chance of life. He rolled over and over down the rocky slope, so that the second rifle slug cut up a spurt of dust at the spot where he had been squatting with his friend. As he rolled, he snatched out his heavy pistol from its holster, and, bringing up short, threw the gun hastily to firing position, and pulled his trigger. The bullet cut the ridge top close to the murderer silhouetted there, spitting fragments of lead over his body.

In the ragged hills, the explosions echoed back and forth, finally dying off in the distance.

But the accuracy of rifle over pistol at such range told. At the third shot, the Texan below took a long slug through the brain.

His arm fell limp in front of him as he collapsed.

The killer hastily rose, ramming fresh shells into his Winchester, warm from the deadly work it had done.

He pulled up the bandanna around his

neck to hide his face until only the red-glinting eyes were visible under the low-pulled Stetson.

"Have to move 'em," he muttered. "I can't leave 'em there!"

He worked back to his saddled horse, standing at the foot of the sage-covered ridge from which he had done his killings. The sound of approaching men caused him to wait, alert. But then he nodded, shoved his horse on.

He had recognized those oncoming riders — his own men, though he did not ride at their head.

A big hombre with stringy black hair, a jutting, black-bearded chin, and long, bony legs, rode at the head of half a dozen other tough-looking devils. A crooked grin showed his tobacco-stained buck teeth as he rode up.

"That you shootin', Boss?" he demanded.

"Yeah, Tank," the killer snapped shortly. "And I've cut out some work for yuh to do. Hustle! Work over to that next ridge and pick up the two bodies yuh'll find there. Fetch 'em to me, and their hosses as well."

"All right," the man called "Tank" growled. "C'mon, boys."

He swung his rangy black horse with the mastery of the plainsman. Guns rode in his holsters, and he had a rifle in the boot under one leg. Like his companions he wore a buckskin jacket, leather pants, and a brown Stetson.

His eyes, which had a greenish tint to them, were set close together over his sharp-bridged nose that had been broken in some brawl.

The man Tank had spoken to as "Boss," the heartless devil who had killed in such cold blood, rolled a brown cigarette, and lighted it, watching the trail until the gang he had sent on the merciless errand returned, bringing the corpses of his victims. Then he drew a hunting knife from the sheath at his back ribs, and in a minute had completed his grisly work. He had scalped the two dead men!

The desperadoes who rode the outlaw trail under Tank Loman stared and shook their heads. They were not shocked, but they did not understand the purpose of this.

"So yuh're takin' scalps, now, huh?" Loman remarked, with a snaggle-toothed grin.

The boss shrugged impatiently, but did not answer the question. "All right," was all he said. "We'll dump this carrion a couple of miles down the valley."

Tank Loman pushed back his sweated Stetson to scratch his straggly-locked head.

"Yuh want 'em to figger the Comanches got 'em?" he asked, as though a bright light dawned.

"Yes, yes," the boss said impatiently. "C'mon! Let's start 'fore some more come along."

South on a rough, rocky trail that wound up and down over the wild hills, they rode. After a quick run, the boss pulled up and gave a short order.

"Drop 'em," he snapped.

The bodies were thrown roughly onto the ground near the trail where no further heed was paid to them.

The leader straightened in his saddle and glowered at the valley, spreading for miles north and south, watered by mountain creeks and a brown river. Here and there smoke from stone chimneys columned into the clear Texas air. The tangy scent of creosote and sage made the air a delight to inhale.

Houses and other buildings of small spreads were scattered through the valley, the homes of settlers come to this remote spot in the hope of finding peace after the horrors of the Civil War had sickened men's souls. Men who had fought on the losing side had come here, trying to find peace for their souls in which had burned the bitter

12

gall of humiliating defeat.

"They must go," muttered the boss. "Every one of them."

Such men as he cared nothing for the death and destruction his evil designs might bring upon innocent people.

Such men cared less for human anguish.

"S'pose they won't?" Tank Loman asked.

"They will — or die! Now looka here, Tank, them two hombres I just potted nearly ruined my plan. Can't take no more chances. You put a couple of men on guard up there, in case any more happen along, savvy? Make shore all sign's wiped out."

They turned back toward the northwest, leaving the valley.

"Reckon they musta been chasin' wild cattle when they come there," Loman suggested as they rode on.

The boss nodded. He looked back over his hunched shoulder, and his brow blackened.

"I'll rout 'em all out," he repeated, and it was an evil promise.

A man riding in the van of the horsemen, topping a rise, turned and galloped back to the chiefs.

"Hossman comin'," he reported. "Down from north."

"Who is it?" the leader asked sharply.

"Dunno. Never seen him before, Boss. But he rides like a soldier."

"Hide, then," came the quick command. "Pull off the trail. We don't want to be recognized."

The informant shook his head.

"I reckon he's already glimpsed me, Boss," he demurred.

The leader cursed. "Fool! Then we'll have to take care of him."

Riding in from the northern wilderness to hit the valley trail, the oncoming man seemed interested only in the sign that lay before him. The pace of the rangy dun he was mounted on grew slower and slower. Time and again the man, after scrutinizing the trail sign, would glance up toward the rocky rise where the ambushed killers lay in wait for him, but if he was in any way aware of their presence, he gave no sign.

The rider Captain Robert Pryor, formerly of the Union Army, spoke softly, aloud, to Saber, his mouse-colored horse with the black stripe along his back that was his constant companion.

"Saber, them blood drops we see on the ground are fresh. Shod hosses been here, too. And why'd that hombre duck back that-away when he saw us comin'?"

The line of Pryor's bronzed chin was set,

14

firm. His blue eyes were earnest, shot with a devil-may-care courage, however, for such a situation as this confronting him was familiar enough. That was natural for a man who had been a scout for General George A. Custer against the great cavalry of Jeb Stuart, Confederate leader.

Now that the Civil War was over Pryor, known along the Border where his home had been as the "Rio Kid," had not lost the cunning he had learned during his scouting days in the army when a false move had meant instant death. Rather had his work in the wilds accentuated this keenness of perception. Hostile Indians roamed the hills and plains; highwaymen lurked in the bush. Only by constant vigilance could a man hope to survive, to win.

And little ever escaped the bright keen eyes of the Rio Kid.

"My rib wound's twingin', Saber," he muttered. "That shore means trouble."

The Kid wore leather chaps to protect his legs from the barbs of chaparral and bush. The wide Stetson he wore to shield eyes from the brilliant sun was cocked over his crisp chestnut hair.

Broad at the shoulders, the Rio Kid's body tapered to narrow hips, and his was the ideal weight for a cavalryman.

A carbine was strapped under his leg and, slung across his chest were two cartridge belts, one to supply the brace of Colt pistols visible in holsters and the two hidden revolvers sheathed under his armpits, and the other loops filled with ammunition for the carbine. Such a man, so outfitted like a one-man arsenal, was always prepared for a jam, and in this country he might be caught in one anywhere, any time. With the firearms he had ready he could deliver thirty shots before he was forced to stop and reload.

Such precautions were necessary when a man might at any time be attacked by Indians or marauding outlaw gangs.

No twinge of fear excited the Rio Kid now, though the tonic of danger, a pleasure to him, caused his eyes to glow as he worked out the problem confronting him. He did not have any known enemies in this section of Texas.

The men he was sure were awaiting his approach might be a robber band, though, watching the trail for travelers.

Dust showed on man and horse, for they had come a long way. That was not usual for Bob Pryor, for through his army training and natural bent he was scrupulously neat about his gear and clothes. His guns, with which he had grown expert from childhood and during the Civil War, gleamed in the light however. His leather was oiled and in good repair. A single glance at him showed power, the strength of a leader of men.

"S'pose we prick 'em up a little and have some fun," he suggested to the dun.

Saber quivered along his black stripe, instinctively understanding. He, too, enjoyed a scrap. Fierce and untamed, inclined to kick and bite at strangers, the mustang was always gentle with Pryor and proved that he had been carefully trained — though distinctly a one-man horse.

Saber was very long of leg, and not at all prepossessing in appearance; he was inclined to be bony and had a bad temper except with his master and with those his owner ordered him to treat with respect. But though Saber did not look like a racer, he could outrun anything on four legs with which the Kid had come in contact, either during the Civil War or since, on the Border. In battle Saber was an equine devil, fighting with hoofs and teeth. And as comrades Saber and the Rio Kid were two fighters who understood each other.

"Have to take care of Celestino, first," Pryor muttered.

He swung the dun's head, trotting back

along the rough road. His light whistle was answered, and another rider rounded the turn to join him.

"What ees wrong, General?" called Celestino Mireles, the handsome young Mexican who was always sure to be somewhere near where the Rio Kid was to be found.

The slim Mexican boy — for he was still in his teens — turned his eager brown face to his friend and mentor. He had the countenance of an immature Spanish grandee, with curved lips, and aquiline nose. Jet-black hair showed under his fancy sombrero. His velvet clothing was of a dark-red color, and in the wide sash wound about his slender body he had stuck his arsenal — pistols and the long knife loved by Mexicans.

Pryor had saved the lad from horrible death at the hands of the Eagle, leader of a robber band on the Rio Grande, who had swooped down on the Mireles' *hacienda.* The death of young Mireles' father, the wiping out of his close friends, had left the boy at a loose end. The worship he offered the Kid was that of a young brother. In spite of Pryor's protests he had chosen to ride the danger trail with the Rio Kid whom he called "General" and to whom he had sworn allegiance.

18

"Yuh note the trail, Celestino?" drawled Pryor, with a nod over his shoulder.

"*Si,* General. Blood. Half a dozen men — shod horses."

"Good. Yuh're learnin', *amigo mio.* They're lyin' up ahead, and I figger they're waitin' for us. Follow me, now, and we'll see why they're hidin' so."

The Mexican smiled.

Pryor turned the dun westward off the main trail into the valley. Saber dug in his hoofs to climb to a high point, the Mexican's handsome black mare following. From the point they reached they could see over the ridge and hunt for the lurking foe the Kid's keen senses had discovered.

Bob Pryor, the Rio Kid, had no idea what the purpose of the hidden men ahead might be but it seemed fairly certain their intent was not friendly, he was too wary to ride into ambush. Instincts and senses — sight, hearing, smell, touch — combined to tell him that the trail sign meant danger.

He hummed Saber's favorite tune as he drew up to watch the other ridge:

Said the big black charger
To the little white mare,
The sergeant claims yore feed bill
Really ain't fair —

19

"General, I see zem!" Celestino called softly.

The Kid, too, observed the Stetson top that indicated their location. The next moment a masked face stealthily peeked up over a rock and light scintillated on a bright Winchester rifle barrel.

Pryor jerked Saber's rein and the dun reared, slid back around a huge boulder, a boulder flecked with rusty red patches. The rifle slug drove into the rocky dirt, spitting up fragments as Saber crowded up against Celestino's mount.

"Keep down," cautioned Pryor. "We've flanked 'em and they don't like it."

"See zose cows run, General, at the shots!" Celestino exclaimed.

Out of a draw to the west galloped a bunch of long-horned, half-wild steers, tails high as they headed for safer parts.

The thunder of hoofs shook the hillside.

The Kid nodded. "Plenty of beeves in these parts, Celestino. They shore multiplied durin' the war and they've gone wild, but a little fattenin' up and they'll bring plenty."

"*Si*, General, zey can be tame' and fatten'. What zey call zat trail from Kansas?"

"Chisholm Trail, Celestino. A half-breed Cherokee Indian named Jesse Chisholm laid it out from Kansas. That was a big herd we met up in north Texas. The East wants beef, if only yuh can get it to where yuh can ship it."

That first shot, sent from the hidden outlaws, did not finish their attempts on the lives of these two riders. Another came the instant the Rio Kid stopped speaking. That second shot was a signal for a fusillade. Bullets whirled in their direction, smashing against the red boulder, ricocheting, hunting Pryor.

"Stick here and hold the hosses," ordered the Rio Kid. "I'm goin' out and sting 'em back."

He slipped from his leather, and crept around the great rock, from which point he could have some shelter and still return the fire. His guns roared as he aimed at exposed hats and shoulders, at puffs of smoke as the men beyond bobbed up and down to shoot.

CHAPTER II:
DANGER VALLEY

The Rio Kid's Colt banged again and again,
echoing through the hills. He did not shoot
fast, but each shot he sent meant what it
said. A man screeched in agony as a slug
tore a hole in his shoulder, and an instant
later a howl went up from another outlaw.

The accuracy of Pryor's pistol work forced
the whole outlaw band to duck down, stay
under cover. They ceased shooting, no man
daring to show himself in the face of the
Kid's display of marksmanship.

Pryor shrugged, and worked his way back
to his Mexican friend and the horses.

"No point in keepin' this up, Celestino,"
he said. "If they're robbers, we'll ride
around 'em."

Mounting Saber, he led the way west,
making sure that ridges of rock interposed
between them and the enemy. Saber
snorted, trying to turn and go back and
fight it out, just for the sport.

"Zey come, General," Celestino called to Bob Pryor.

The Kid glanced back over his shoulder and saw a number of masked men whooping it up on his trail. He turned the dun, and began sending bullets back, Celestino firing with him.

The masked outlaws slowed, and one clutched at his arm. It was plain that they dared not approach too closely. The way the Rio Kid's bullets sang about them discouraged them. The Kid rode on with his young friend.

After a mile of this chase, the gang stopped, apparently ready to give up. They sent a last burst of bullets after Pryor and Celestino Mireles, then swung and headed back the way they had come.

"It's gettin' late," Pryor said, as the last of the pursuers disappeared. "Reckon we'll camp, Celestino."

There was a brook down below and they rode down to it. They watered the horses, took what liquid they needed for themselves and, following Pryor's usual caution in strange country, and the habits of frontiersmen whenever Indians were around, they retired a half mile from the stream. There they rolled up in their blankets in a bush clump. The horses were allowed to roam and graze. There was a full moon and the Rio Kid was continually keeping in mind the fact that this was when the Comanches best liked to raid. . . .

At sunrise the Kid and his young Mexican follower arose. They ate more hardtack and jerked venison, washed down with cool water. Saber came when Pryor whistled a few bars of "Said the Big Black Charger." Saddling up, the Kid caught the black mare for Celestino and together they worked back to the trail he had been following south to the Rio Grande.

Proceeding from where they had left off when interrupted by the ambushers the afternoon before, they found the spot deserted. Farther down the great valley, where they could see many bunches of longhorn cattle, they sighted a group of men.

Not knowing who they might be, and instantly alert and ready, the Rio Kid approached. The men were armed, and they turned to see who was coming, with the frontiersman's wariness. Drawing nearer to them Pryor could see that they were Texans, the sort of folks among whom he had been born and bred. Hardship and privation had lined their faces that were seared by sun and wind. Lean, hard of muscle, their souls, too, were grim, but each had held hard to the hope that in this new land would come new opportunities.

Most of them had fought on the Confederate side during the war. Now Ulysses S. Grant, the victor, hero of Vicksburg, the Wilderness and Appomattox, the soldier who had defeated their great hero Robert E. Lee, was President of the United States. Their hopes were dying, or dead. Carpetbaggers had come from the North to rule them. Their currency was useless, and the losers in the terrible fraternal strife had come home to find chaos and ruin.

"Howdy, gents," sang out the Rio Kid.

An older man returned his greeting, and the courteous salute of Celestino who had been trained to Old World politeness by his dead father, the Don.

"Howdy, suh," the Texan replied.

He was a handsome Southern gentleman with cropped goatee and mustache touched with silver, as was his hair. He had eyes that looked at a man steadily, and carried his straight shoulders like a soldier. Obviously the leader of the other men, the way he spoke to them proved his officer's training. The Rio Kid observed the man's left leg was missing, an oak stump serving in its place. Lost in the war, of course, Pryor decided.

"Colonel White, should we dig the graves here, suh?" inquired a peaceful young Texan when greetings had been exchanged. "Or fetch the bodies down the valley?"

"We'll tote 'em home and bury 'em," ordered Colonel White, with a heavy sigh. "The Comanches got 'em, I reckon. Scalped, hosses stole. Herb, see to tyin' 'em on them ponies."

His eyes were slightly moist.

Herb, the stalwart young man who had spoken, signaled some of the other men and set about picking up the dead men that the Rio Kid had seen lying on the ground as soon as he had ridden up.

"Grab the shoulders, Dave," he said to one of them.

"Okay, Malcom," another young fellow replied.

Herb Malcom was tall, over six feet, with a wide-shouldered body and long, strong limbs. He had tow-colored hair curling over the tanned brow which showed a pleasing space between his brown eyes. Clad in leather, with his Stetson held by a strap under his chin, he efficiently directed the fastening of the dead on the backs of standing horses.

Colonel Amos White turned to the Rio Kid as if he believed a word of explanation necessary.

"Don't s'pose yuh know anything much 'bout these scalpin's we have down here, suh," he said. "The Comanches nip at our flanks every so often, damn their red hides!"

He seemed to like the Rio Kid's looks.

"My name's Bob Pryor, Colonel," the Kid said promptly. "This young feller's Celestino Mireles of Chihuahua, who rides with me. We're jest down from Kansas."

"Yuh crossed Indian Territory, then?" asked the colonel.

"Yes, suh. Swam the Red River at the station. We're headin' home to the Rio."

"Light down with us and spend some time, Pryor — and yuh, too, Celestino," the colonel invited heartily. "Yuh're powerful welcome. My name's White — Amos White."

The Kid and Mireles thanked him with the exaggerated politeness of the times, and accepted the proffered hospitality.

Pryor rode beside Amos White at the head of the cavalcade which took the bodies of the murdered men down the valley. A few brief questions served to inform the Rio Kid that the colonel was the chief of the community, head of the group of Southerners who had invaded the wilderness in the hope of making a new start in life.

There were many young men among them, but other older men, also, the fathers of families. They had been officers in Lee's army. Their homesteads were built of raw timber and rough stone, and here they had tried to remake their lives after the war's ruin, unaware that already a hidden, sinister enemy menaced them with destruction.

The Rio Kid had kept his own counsel about the gang he had run into, and also what his keen scout's eyes had noted. He awaited an opportune moment in which to mention his suspicions about who had murdered the men they were so sadly taking home. The settlers seemed to take it for granted that Indians had attacked the two cowboys dumped on the trail, and after all, the Kid had no proof that this was not true.

In the golden sunlight, Rose Valley looked at peace, and glowed with a hazy beauty. Timber stands of pine and oak, of other valuable woods covered the mountainsides. There was plenty of water for the stock, wild steers and mustangs which had bred and developed in Texas during the war. Game, deer and birds, ran the trails, and the buffalo still migrated to the Staked Plain, westward of Rose Valley, running with thunderous hoofs across the rolling prairies of the West.

Rose Valley ran roughly north and south, widening at the center. The brown river curled in and out along its rocky bed.

Colonel Amos White's ranch was set near the river edge on a flat. It was a little larger than the other homes, though of one story as were the others, and the walls were of thick logs which would stop an Indian arrow or bullet.

Women in homespun dresses, children wearing rough handmade shirts, had collected in the yard, watching the riders as they returned with the missing cowmen.

A wail rose as a woman recognized her dead husband. A mother fainted at sight of her murdered son.

A young woman in a blue dress came out, and looked up at Colonel White inquiringly. The Rio Kid, silently observing, saw that she was beautiful despite the crudely made garment she wore. She had dark hair and deep-blue eyes, a well shaped nose and full red lips. Small, she was formed with a symmetry which has attracted men since the days of Eve.

"Get back inside, Betsy," Colonel White ordered gruffly. "No sight for you to be lookin' on, honey."

Betsy White shook her head, sadness in her lovely face. She was not more than eighteen, the Kid decided, a girl just blossoming to womanhood. Then he noticed Herb Malcom's face as the young fellow watched Betsy. There was a glowing light in Malcom's eyes, and the Rio Kid did not need to be the shrewd reader of men he was to realize that Malcom was in love with the girl.

"Can't hardly blame him, at that," he muttered.

Betsy, too, was aware of Malcom's eyes. She studiously avoided catching his gaze as she went over and tried to offer comfort to the bereaved mother and wife.

Pryor and his loyal follower, Celestino Mireles, dismounted, unsaddled, and turned their tired horses into a corral.

They looked about as they strode over to the kitchen to get some grub, real cooked food after the long weeks on the trail.

"General," remarked Celestino, his voice low, "zese people — zey are poor."

Captain Pryor nodded. He had noted the scarcity of necessary supplies. They had plenty of meat, and they could raise a little wheat for flour. But of other things, the Rose Valley people were bereft. Painful attempts to make the best of it showed everywhere, in their house furnishings, gear and clothing. They were in desperate need of money.

The meal offered them consisted of beef and a warm drink made of water and burnt cereal.

That evening the other settlers from round about gathered at Colonel White's to hear the news brought from the outside world by Pryor and Celestino. Few visitors came to the isolated valley, and scraps of information were hoarded.

There were strong men here, men who had lost their Cause. Faces showed lean and bitter in the ruby glow of the fire that crackled in the stone outdoor hearth.

The Rio Kid's voice, still touched with the Texan drawl despite his years in the North, held them spellbound as he gave an account of what was going on in the outside world.

"That's mighty interestin', suh," remarked Colonel White, during a pause. "But I reckon such things ain't for us. The carpet-baggers got our state in their grip and the iron heel has ground us down. Yuh look like a soldier yoreownself. Would it be too presumin' if I asked did yuh ride for Jeb Stuart? Yuh got all the earmarks of a good cavalryman."

All eyes fixed the Rio Kid, squatted in the

center of the circle.

"I was a cavalryman, Colonel," he replied, his voice gentle, "but not for Jeb Stuart, who was one of the best. I rode for General Custer."

A stunned silence fell on them. Women's eyes grew frightened, and several of the men dropped their hands toward their pistols.

"A traitor!" a hot-headed ex-officer growled. "He fought for the damned Yankees!"

The Rio Kid fixed the challenger with an unblinking stare. "Why, suh, that's where yuh're wrong," he said calmly. "Every man fought in the war as his inside self told him. Mine said stay with the Union. Now the war's over and done with, though, and there's no need for folks to be enemies no more."

The stately Colonel White rose to his feet and balanced himself on his wooden leg.

"This gentleman," he said courteously, "is our guest. There's sense in what he says, though a man may think as he likes."

Pryor was sorry for these people, his own kind. He knew the bitterness rankling in their hearts. He wished with all his heart to help them, and pondered a way.

He went on talking, then, as though nothing had happened to disturb the party.

"The railroad's bein' built through Kansas right now," he informed them gravely. "It's already touched Abilene, Kansas. Why, a few months ago this here Abilene was nothin' but a few shacks on the creek; now it's a city, with pens for thousands of cows. Yuh see, the East wants beef. On our way down we run into several herds drivin' north on the trail Jesse Chisholm made when he run them Indians to the Territory for the Government. There's money in cows, a fortune. These hills round here are filled with money, gents — four-hoofed cash."

"He's right!" cried the colonel. "We are fools, boys, sittin' here stewin' while we ought to be drivin' beef to Kansas. It's a great idea."

"But how we goin' to reach this here Chisholm Trail?" a more cautious Texan objected. "And how'll we savvy the way to Kansas? It's a mighty long pull with cows."

"I was thinkin'," Pryor replied, "that I'm footloose and fancy free, gents. I'd be glad enough to show yuh the way. We can drive from here to Red River Station and cross into the Territory there. I'll scout the trail for yuh."

Excitement seized upon them, as they saw a way out of their difficulties. Their enmity disappeared and questions were showered upon the Kid.

"Yuh'll need supplies and plenty of guns, in case of Indian trouble," Pryor advised.

Colonel White's face fell.

"We haven't any money, Pryor," he said apologetically. "We've been worried 'bout gettin' enough cash to buy up the range we need round the valley."

"Yuh ought to be able to borrow enough to grubstake yore drive," said the Kid. "Once yuh reach Kansas with yore beef, yuh can sell it at big profit."

Colonel White gave his one good leg a resounding slap.

"Dog my cats if I don't try it!" he exclaimed. "I'll ride to Piketown tomorrer and see John Barrett — he's the merchant there. Herb, you take charge of collectin' the best cows yuh can outa the hills. Every man who can ride will help yuh."

"Don't forget to brand 'em," cautioned the Kid. "Road brand and ear marks, too."

CHAPTER III:
GRUBSTAKE

Enthusiasm for the Rio Kid's idea swept away any lingering touch of enmity they had felt when they had found that he had fought in the Union Army. The settlers of Rose Valley went to bed with visions of a new fortune to dream about.

Bob Pryor drew Colonel White aside, as they prepared to retire for the night.

"Colonel," he said, "I didn't say nothin' before, figgerin' mebbe it'd all come out in the wash. But about them two dead men yuh brought home. Mebbe yuh didn't take a careful look at the trail, huh?"

"Why no, I didn't," the colonel admitted. " 'Twas right rocky where they lay. And plain the Comanches got 'em. What else coulda done for 'em in jest that awful way?"

"The men who shot and scalped 'em," the Rio Kid declared, "were not Indians. They rode shod hosses, for one thing. For another, I'm right shore it was them same killers I had a little brush with the evenin' 'fore yuh rode out and found yore scalped cowboys."

"White men done it?" The colonel's eyes were unbelieving.

"Yes, suh. But why? Have yuh any enemies in these parts? Robbers or outlaws or other bandits who might injure yore folks?"

"Robbers?" Colonel White laughed bitterly. "What have we got that robbers'd want? No money, no belongin's worth stealin', Rio Kid." The colonel used Pryor's nickname with a slight smile. He liked the name — had liked it ever since Captain Pryor had told him that was how he was usually known along the Border.

"As for cows," the colonel went on, "why there's plenty of 'em roamin' wild to take. Hosses as well."

The Rio Kid nodded. Celestino Mireles was already rolled in his blanket, asleep. The Kid said good night to White, and went to join his young friend beneath the trees some distance from the log house. The mystery of the scalped Texans must wait for solution. . . .

Some time during the dark hours the Rio Kid woke with a start, woke to the instant alertness of his trained senses, seeing the moon-bathed scene with the White homestead a black bulk nearby. His hand was already upon his Colt pistol butt as he came up, his lithe muscles ready for action.

A sound close at hand sent his glance that way. It was a familiar enough noise, the scrape of a horse's hoofs upon the ground. And there was Saber, the dun with the black stripe down his back, approaching him.

"What's wrong, Saber?" the Kid whispered.

The rangy dun nuzzled his friend's hand, sniffing his warning. And, as the Rio Kid straightened up, he caught the heavy thudding of many horses galloping through the valley.

"Celestino!"

Pryor nudged the Mexican youth with his boot toe. The boy was at once awake, clutching his knife.

"Get yore hoss!" warned Pryor. "Indians might be attackin'!"

He leaped on Saber's back, and then quickly fired three shots, close together, as a warning. That was the usual warning among the people of the frontier.

The Rio Kid's shots roused up the White household. He heard calls from inside, and caught the flicker of a light as he swept out on the dun to intercept the approaching band of night riders.

They were coming hell-for-leather up the valley. Then he heard screams, and gunshots, and knew they must have attacked the cabins on their way in.

Saber snorted, quivered along his black stripe, eager for the fray. The Kid, coolly watching the shadowy figures come on, saw a bunched gang of horsemen. The bushes threw black shadow bands across the rough road that passed through the valley. Then, to the south, he caught a rising red glow in the sky — fire, a burning habitation!

"Halt!" Pryor cried, as he faced the onrushing horsemen.

His reply was a fusillade that whistled about his ears and snapped at the clothing of his body. He whirled Saber, turning off for cover to the west, firing at the attackers to stop them.

They swerved, and he glimpsed an Indian chief, with full feather headdress, his face a blue of black and red stains, and buckskins covering his big body. Unearthly whoops rang up from the throats of the night attackers as they spurred onward.

As they approached the White place, however, the colonel and his men, roused by the Rio Kid's shots, were already in shooting position, concealed in the shadows and by the buildings. Buffalo guns roared their *whooshing* explosions in the darkness, flashing fire for several feet as they vomited the heavy slugs. A night rider set up a horrible screaming, clutching the mane of his horse as he bent over in the saddle, wounded.

Down the valley a woman was wailing, her screams rising above the yells and shouts. The burning cabin sent a ruby glow up into the night sky.

The Rio Kid's pistols were hammering at the flank of the riders as they whirled northward. Saber, snorting in the excitement, sniffing at the acrid odor of burnt powder, which he had grown to love during his days as a war charger, danced toward the foe.

But they did not stop, since the volleys from White's place told them the settlers were fully awake and ready for them. Hoarse shouts came to the Kid's ears, the confusion of such a night fight.

He swung the dun onto the road, the shod hoofs striking sparks from the stones as Saber galloped in pursuit. The giant Indian chief, in the van, was leading the retreat, for through the Kids alert action, the attack had changed from onslaught to a getaway.

Dust rose, sending an obscuring cloud up in the wake of the swift moving mustangs which the attackers rode. They whirled on north, out of Rose Valley, and the Rio Kid, after running them for a half mile, nipping at their heels, swung Saber and returned.

He found the White homestead lighted by tallow lamps, home-made affairs shaped from pewter by hand, and burning animal fat. These Texans could not afford real lamps and the fuel to burn in them, and reduced fats to use for light. They gave a smoky yellow flame and permeated the rooms with an unpleasant odor.

The Rose Valley pioneers had come rushing to the colonel's home. Two men had been shot down at the south of the settlement, the Rio Kid learned, but only one house had been fired.

"It was Indians," growled Major Young, a tough-hided Texan who had been a Confederate officer during the war. "I seen the chief."

The stunning attack depressed everybody, but in such a land and at such a time these people were hardened to death and Indian outrages. The dead were buried, the widows taken in by kindly neighbors, and life went on, after a fashion.

An hour later Rose Valley, save for posted guards to watch for return of the night marauders, was again sleeping. . . .

In the morning Colonel White, Bob Pryor, Celestino Mireles, Major Young and four older valley men, all of them former officers of the Confederate army, saddled up and started for Piketown. The settlement lay forty miles from Rose Valley, in a south easterly direction.

Saber, none too friendly toward strange horses, which he liked to bully with nips and lashing of his hoofs, was out ahead, carrying the Rio Kid, who scouted the trail. They rode through the morning at as fast a clip as Amos White could manage, staying together. The sun rose, higher and higher into the sky, beating its rays down hotly on the Rio Kid's heavy Stetson.

The scout was following the bank of a small river which, the Kid had been told, passed by Piketown, when a dust cloud showed ahead. Pryor pushed on, and met three cowmen, one a broad-shouldered, stocky hombre with leather jacket and heavy chaparejos to guard against the chaparral thorns. He was young, in his early twenties, wearing a thick mustache over his strong lips.

Skyblue eyes fixed the Rio Kid as the latter pulled up at the trio's signal. The wild mustangs danced, held down by the masterly skill of their riders, as the horsemen talked.

"Howdy, Mister," the young leader said in his deep voice.

He was dust-covered and his face lined with alkali showed that his ride had been long.

"Howdy, suh," the Rio Kid replied gravely.

"My name's Chisum — John Chisum," the man in the middle of the trio said. "We're ridin' ahead of one of my cattle herds. Yuh'll have to pull outa the trail and give us way. Otherwise yuh might stampede my cows."

"Glad to do that, Chisum," the Rio Kid replied, and smilingly remarked, "I cut one of yore herds last week, further north."

Chisum nodded. The light of the empire builder glowed in his youthful eyes. To the Rio Kid it was plain that here was a trail-opener, a man who was to own more cattle than any of his peers.

Chisum slung a leg round the horn of his saddle, rolling himself a crude cigarette. He wiped the dust from his bronzed face.

"Got a contract to supply the Gov'ment with beef for the reservation Injuns in New Mexico, Mister," he said, pride in his voice. "I'm movin' all my herds to that country."

"Yuh drivin' to Kansas at all?" asked the

Kid eagerly.

"No. I'm headin' west."

The breeze brought to them a heavy lowing, the noise a trail herd makes as it moves. Chisum glanced back over his shoulder, nodded to his companions, and said good-by to Pryor.

"Stay outa their way, Mister," he warned again and, with a wave, he spurred on west.

The Kid turned Saber and galloped back to join his friends. He led them north to a high point from which they could look down and see the passing herd.

There were a couple of thousand animals in this herd of John Chisum's. At the front rode a couple of point men, with flankers strung at strategic intervals, and with more riders, their bandannas up to ward off the worst of the choking dust, bringing up the drag. The cows, long-horned, half wild beasts, moved slowly along, the stronger animals in front, with here and there only a single steer in line. They bunched up into groups, forming a straggling, uneven advance, a line that extended back for a mile or more.

"That's the way it's done," Pryor remarked to the Texans, who stared at the passing herd, taking in the details, for none of them had ever seen a cattle drive before.

"We'll do it, dog my cats if we don't!" exclaimed Major Young. "Kid, yuh've saved our bacon for us. We can make enough money on this Kansas drive to cinch our land titles and buy what we jest got to have to keep on livin'."

New hope glowed in the eyes of the downtrodden Texans. Eagerly they shoved on toward Piketown.

It was the middle of the afternoon when they rode down into the town, set on a flat along the north bank of the river. The buildings were of unpainted timber, shacks set about an open space called the plaza. Goats and cows and pigs grazed as they liked on this common. The road was rutted, the intense sun having dried out the mud.

There were two saloons, and a general store marked with a crude sign over its wooden awning:

JOHN BARRETT
Merchandise

"Barrett's a Yankee," Amos White informed Pryor, as they dismounted.

The colonel's wooden leg made long riding difficult for him, and now was as stiff as a board from the trip made from Rose Valley.

"I'm hopin' he'll stake us so we can make our cattle drive," he sighed. "He knows us. We've bought what little we could at his store here, and he's been out to Rose Valley once or twice."

They dropped their reins over the continuous hitch-rail, ducked under it and stepped up on the low porch. Barrett's emporium was a large, square building filled with all sorts of goods. There were guns and ammunition, ploughs, saddles, clothing, foods that were not perishable, such as sides of bacon, dried beef, sugar, flour, hardtack, tobacco and candles. The odor of kerosene oil pervaded the place. Sweets, hardware and apparel stood in a confused array in the dark, crowded warehouse.

A young clerk came out from behind a counter as the riders from Rose Valley entered.

"Is John Barrett here?" asked Colonel White.

"Yes, suh, but I think he's sleepin'. I'll see."

Presently a deep voice boomed, "Who's that?" and a man emerged from the rear part of the store, rubbing his eyes.

He was a big fellow with a hearty manner, wearing dark trousers tucked into soft black halfboots, and a white shirt with the sleeves rolled up on brawny arms. He had sandy hair and a sunburned face with seams about his blue eyes.

He smiled a welcome, sticking out a hand to the colonel.

"Why, Colonel!" he cried. "Glad to see yuh, sir. What can I do for yuh? Yuh're quite a stranger in town."

"I'm anxious to have a word with yuh, private, Barrett," Colonel White said with dignity. "Got a proposition to make."

The merchant's eyes narrowed. He was a shrewd trader.

"Well, let's have it, Colonel," he said, and shook his head. "Though these days credit's mighty hard to give."

The Rio Kid trailed after Colonel White and Barrett, into the latter's office at the back. The colonel acted as spokesman, telling of their determination to drive a cattle herd up the Chisholm Trail to Kansas.

John Barrett heard him out. Then he shrugged.

"It's a good idea, Colonel," he admitted. "But what d'yuh want with me?"

"We need guns and ammunition, and saddles," the colonel said promptly. "Also food supplies to carry along, tobacco and the like. Stake us and we'll pay yuh back when we sell our beef."

Barret laughed. "S'posin' Indians attack yuh in the Territory? S'pose a stampede ruins yore herd, Colonel? What then? I'd lose my money."

"No, yuh wouldn't," White declared stoutly. "We'll guarantee to pay yuh even if we fail to make Kansas."

"Yuh'll make it, Colonel," drawled Bob Pryor. "In fact, if Mr. Barrett won't loan yuh enough to go on, I reckon I can dig it up for yuh. Only it'll take a little while for me to reach the Rio and get back."

"Huh," Barrett said, eying the Kid. Then he struck out his hand. "More I think of it, Colonel, the better I like it. I'll stake yuh. Yore credit's good here and yuh pay me later on after yuh sell yore beef."

They shook hands on it. Excitement prevailed when the Texans waiting outside heard the good news. Immediately they set about choosing what might be needed on the drive. The advice of the Rio Kid was sought about each article.

Closeted with John Barrett, Colonel White signed the necessary papers to make the merchant a partner in the proceeding. But Bob Pryor was equally busy, assisting the ranchers in making their purchases.

CHAPTER IV:
DRIVE

Young Herb Malcom took Betsy White's
small hand in his work-hardened grip, and
looked into her deep-blue eyes.

"Betsy," he said, his voice low in the darkness, "yuh know they have picked me to be
trail boss, don't yuh? We're goin' to make
money outa this drive to Kansas, and it
means the start of better times for all of us."

Shyly she watched him, her breath quick-
ening. It was good-by, she knew, until Herb
Malcom should come riding back from the
Chisholm Trail.

"You're the best man for it, Herb," she
said softly. "Father leans on you — you
know that. But I — I'll miss you."

"I'll make it," he promised, almost fierce
determination in his low voice. "The Rio
Kid's promised to go all the way through
with us. He's a mighty good man, Betsy,
and he's shore givin' us a new lease on life.
At first I was mad when I found out he'd

fought on the Northern side. But he's right. That's over and done with and we're all Americans together."

"He's a fine man," Betsy agreed. "And so are you, Herb."

In the shadows near her father's home, she let Malcom take her in his arms, and kiss her full red lips. It was a kiss of betrothal.

"You'll come ridin' back as soon as you can, won't you?" she asked softly, touching his cheek with her hand.

"I swear I will," he told her with determination. "I'll be back jest as soon as those cows are sold. We can start life right together, Betsy."

At last they parted, the man's long strides taking him from the girl, and her white face showing in the darkness as she stood watching him till he disappeared down the road.

Herb Malcom must be up at crack of dawn next morning. All preparations had been made during the past days for the all-important drive to Kansas. Provisions had been packed — necessary food to give the men strength in the arduous work they must do throughout the long journey north. Saddles and gear were in the best shape, and every man who could fork a bronc had been busy rounding up, picking the best of the Rose Valley herds, branding and road-marking the cattle that were to go.

Red streamers showed in the east as Herb Malcom, in leather jacket and chaps, high boots bought at John Barrett's Piketown store, a new rifle under one long leg, .45 Colts in holsters at his hips, Stetson strapped straight under his determined chin, took the point and gave the signal for the start of the great cattle drive.

At various spots, north of the valley, bunches of cows were being held by other cowboys to be run into the passing herd. It would swell to thousands by the time they were joined and ready to blaze a new path through Texas to the start of the Chisholm Trail.

Betsy White and her father, the old colonel, whose wooden leg prevented him from undertaking such an arduous trip as the weeks on the trail would mean, had ridden out to see them off. His job was to hold the fort in the valley, while the younger and stronger men who had been chosen made the drive.

Herb Malcom leaned over in his saddle to kiss Betsy, which was equivalent to an announcement to everybody that they would be married when he returned from Kansas.

It was a scene that was again and again

repeated throughout the decades of the trail driving, not only in great Texas, but through all the wide-flung cow empire. Mothers and sweethearts, fathers and brothers said good-by gaily enough to their loved ones, young fellows in their teens who were eager for the adventure of the drive. Some came back home, many others did not. They dropped from sight, often forever, some killed by Indians or in flooded rivers, others snared in the Northern towns by ties of affection or by business attractions, or joining other expeditions that led them far from home.

Herb Malcom carried Betsy White's kiss in his heart through the danger that came to him. He kept the slim girl's smiling face in a vision as she waved farewell.

Ahead might lie death, or danger far worse than the expected hazards of hostile savages, the elements, sickness. But there was one danger at which they could not even guess — horror plotted in the minds of evil men who sought to destroy the pioneers of Rose Valley. . . .

"Push 'em hard the first few days, Malcom," ordered Bob Pryor, the Rio Kid, as he walked Saber, the dun, beside the young leader's chestnut mount. "That'll get 'em tired so they won't be so all-fired ready to stampede if somebody drops a pin. Then they'll be broke to drivin', and off their reg'lar range. They'll be restless till they get used to this."

They had joined the various herd sections, and back of them, for over a mile, strung three thousand longhorns, full-grown stock that would fetch the best price at Abilene, Kansas, center of the cattle shipping world at that moment.

Up out of the great valley now, they were crossing a grassy plateau, with the Texas sun yellow as gold overhead. Rose Valley lay a few miles southwest as they headed the herd for the Red River and the crossing at the station.

The Rio Kid looked as fresh as though just out of a bandbox. With his accoutrements meticulously shined, the metal of his guns caught the brilliant light. His leather was darkly smooth and well oiled. A waterproof was rolled to the inch-fraction at his saddle cantle; the army carbine with its short-nosed barrel, at regulation angle.

His clean, bronzed face was set, the devil-may-care blue eyes glinting with his reckless courage, a nerve which had communicated itself to the lost people of Rose Valley. They had taken him at his word and were following him to fortune. He rode with the genius of the trained cavalryman and Westerner, correct in every detail, from the crisp, close-cropped hair that showed from beneath his Stetson to his shining guns. His passion for neatness would have made it possible for him to pass the most exacting inspection even on the wild plains.

Saber's eyes rolled wickedly as he took a tentative bite at the big horse Herb Malcom was riding. The animal shied.

"Easy, now, Saber," the Rio Kid chided his pet. "This is no time for that. Yuh'll scare them cows. On this trip yuh gotta act like a gentleman."

Saber's black stripe quivered as he seemed to shrug off that advice.

Malcom speeded up the pace, trotting his horse. The flankers, strung out on either side of the cattle lines, began to push the animals a bit faster. Young Celestino Mireles, who "had a way with critters," was riding flank, expertly turning back bulls or cows which tried to break away from the groupings.

The thousands on thousands of hoofs, running back for a mile and a half, cut up the earth and sent billows of dust into the clear sky. In the drag cowboys drew up their bandannas to keep from choking, as the sticky alkaline dust sifted up to cover them from Stetson to spur. And half a mile behind the last group of steers came pack horses carrying food supplies, and a hundred spare horses for the cowmen.

Twenty-five men made up the herders. They were mostly unmarried young fellows. Here and there were ex-officers of Lee's and Stonewall Jackson's brigades, older men who could be spared from the valley.

"I'll get out ahead and scout the best route, Malcom," the Rio Kid said, as the world seemed to thunder with myriad hoofs. "We'll drive till sundown, and then bed down for the night."

He nodded and, with a quick wave, urged Saber out in front, soon leaving the van of the cattle drive behind him.

The country rolled out before him in a grand sweep that was breath-taking. The Kid whistled "Said the Big Black Charger," for Saber's benefit, the dun cocking his ear to that familiar tune, which he would always answer, from as far as he could hear it.

"Feelin' good, ain't yuh, Saber?" Pryor remarked, touching the spirited animal's warm neck with a soothing hand. "Had a rest while they were gettin' the cows together and yuh're rarin' to go. Well, we might see some fun 'fore we shove these critters into the pens at Abilene. Indians are mighty thick in the Territory."

This was the life Bob Pryor loved — the open space of the great wilderness, its inherent perils, the intoxicating power that a man felt when he conquered, alone against it all. In the Civil War, as an aide-de-camp to General George Armstrong Custer, Captain Pryor had done much advance scouting for the cavalry of the Army of the Potomac. His daring had become famous even among a million daring men.

One leg drawn up a bit as he rode, the Rio Kid figured the best route for the great herd behind him. Whenever he made a turn that might be missed by Herb Malcom he would set a rock where the trail boss would see it and take the right way.

They made twenty miles that first day. Then the Kid chose a camping spot by water, with deep, lush grass for the steers to feed upon during the night, and to bed down on.

"First thing yuh know, Saber," he remarked to his horse, "we'll be tame cowhands."

Around five P.M. the van of the herd came into sight, with Herb Malcom riding point, out a bit ahead of the leaders. Malcom saw Pryor and led the first bunches of cattle to the deep grass along the creek's edge. The bunches began piling up as the herders rode round and round them, winding them into as small a space as possible.

Leaving a few men on guard, the trail hands retired to a nearby hilltop where the cook was preparing supper. They were weary men, dust-covered men, and irritated by the vagaries of the stubborn, half-wild beasts. Threw themselves on the ground to rest.

The Rio Kid squatted beside Herb Malcom as both of them drank coffee from tin mugs.

"So far, so good," he remarked cheerfully. "We'll put a few guards on the first shift, then others can relieve 'em at midnight."

Herb Malcom nodded. His steady eyes sought the back trail. Not so far behind lay Rose Valley and Betsy. Then he looked north, toward the unknown wilderness of Indian Territory. That was the way duty led him.

The hard, dangerous work required all hands to give their best, forgetting self in the trial. Night fell, after they had wolfed their meal. A feeling of loneliness swept over them, but weary muscles cried for sleep. Men rolled in blankets and fell asleep the instant they relaxed.

The Rio Kid, as was his habit, slept apart

from the others. The moon was low in the night sky that was powdered with stars when he woke to the infernal sounds of screeching men and the pounding of hoofs. The men guarding the cattle below were shooting and crying for help.

Pryor sprang to his feet, gun in hand. He whistled a shrill bar of "The Big Black Charger" as he hustled down the slope toward the herd. The cattle were bellowing and beginning to run as cursing men leaped to their feet, throwing off their blankets, following in the Kid's wake.

Whoops rang out, more gunshots roared through the night. Across the river rode the dark shapes of attacking men — Indians, Pryor thought, attempting to stampede the cattle and reach the horses.

Saber came galloping up to his master and the Kid sprang on the dun, bareback, riding toward the disturbance. As he whirled in full-tilt, riding low over the dun's flying mane, he saw one of the trail hands who was on night guard throw up his hands and fall from his mount, caught in the concerted fire of the wild riders coming at them.

The dangerous long horns of the cattle menaced horse and rider as the Rio Kid guided Saber in and out among them, skillfully evading the sharp points of the horns.

Steers were throwing up their tails, snorting, starting to run for it.

Closer and closer to the advancing enemy came the Rio Kid. A shrill warwhoop sent his eyes toward the river bank and along it he saw the giant Indian chieftain with feathers streaming behind him as he rode, dashing at the head of his evil band.

"It's the same gang as hit the valley that night!" he muttered, throwing up his Colt.

Moving cattle interposed between him and the chief. The jolting of the racing dun under him made aim difficult and his target, riding low over a great dark-colored stallion, was moving with the speed of the wind. But the Kid saw the big Indian suddenly rise up, a fractional instant after Pryor had let go his revolver hammer and the firing-pin had struck home, the Colt kicking back against the expert strong hand.

The chief on the stallion veered, plunging down the grassy bank into the water. The Rio Kid, nostrils wide in the excitement of battle, sought to work through the milling herd to catch him as the stallion began swimming in midstream.

CHAPTER V:
ATTACK IN THE NIGHT

Seconds only had elapsed since the Kid reached the herd. Herb Malcom and his boys had grabbed horses and were coming on at full speed.

The band of riders behind the chief swerved as they saw their chief flee, riding straight toward the Rio Kid. A fifteen-hundred-pound bull bumped Saber in the crush, knocking the dun sideward. Then the cows began running down the river bank and suddenly before him the Rio Kid saw the whole gang of raiders who had hit them.

He jerked hard on his reins, and the dun reared up on his hind legs to make the turn. The Kid's Colt snapped furiously at the bunched riders who whooped it up, banging away with devilish intention to kill him.

The sounds of shrieks and cursing rose high over the thundering and bellowing of the running longhorns. His guns in constant action, the Kid had made another hit, and a second night rider left the pack for the river, swimming his horse to safety and disappearing in the alders across the stream.

The fury of Pryor's fighting and the accuracy of his guns took them by surprise, and as they felt the awful bite of his leaden slugs they slowed, pausing for better aim at the elusive target. In the semi-darkness the flash of the heavy guns showed yellow-red, and the explosions echoed from the slopes of the river valley.

As Pryor fell back with whistling lead about his ears, nipping at his Stetson and cutting his leather — one slug bit a groove in his left arm — Herb Malcom and ten of his men came racing their horses in to join the fray. In the gun flashes, they could make out the naked brown chests of the attackers, the dark, painted faces, and the eagle feathers banded about the heads.

"Let 'em have it, boys!" yelled Malcom.

A fusillade from the cowboys turned the attackers. The wounding of their leader, his ignominious flight before the Rio Kid's single-handed fury, had shaken them. Suddenly, with defiant whoops that rent the night, they swung, heading for the water, leaving the scene without the booty they had come to get.

The Kid shoved Saber close to Malcom.

"C'mon!" he ordered. "We got to stop that stampede, 'fore those cows git all the way home!"

They sent a final burst of gunfire after the raiders, and, swinging, the Rio Kid led the way full-tilt after the vanishing herd. As they passed the camp they could see that no one was left there now except the cook. Celestino was nowhere in sight.

"Figger he's ridin' out ahead of the steers with the others, tryin' to turn 'em," muttered Pryor, as they raced on in the chase after the fleeing herd.

Down the valley they galloped, the dust clogging up thick, the trail easy to follow where the great numbers of cattle had crushed the way.

For an hour they rode, stringing out according to the strength and speed of their mounts. Saber, as was usual in a race, had forged out ahead. Ungainly and unprepossessing as the dun looked, Pryor was thinking for the hundredth time that he had never run across another horse that could outrun Saber.

Out in front of that mad conglomeration of huge beeves cowboys rode, nip-and-tuck, just out of reach of the sharp horns. A slip, a false step by a nimble-footed horse, and the rider would be catapulted to horrible death under thousands of tons of blinded, maddened cattle.

Another hour, and they still rode on, but the pace was slackening and the lead cattle began slowly turning up the slope.

Sweat, dirt and blood caked the Rio Kid. Saber at last distanced the other horses and when the Kid passed the riders in the van he saw Celestino and some other Rose Valley herders fighting to turn the cows. Luck had played with them, for the contour of the land had kept most of the herd together. Only a few bunches had broken off from the main herd.

In a daring burst of speed coaxed from the dun, Pryor cut across to the east flank and with his Colt began shooting past the faces of the leading steers. The blinding flashes provided the last urge needed to turn them, and they swung, the great masses behind obeying the herd instinct.

Now, as the break came, Celestino Mireles led the Valley cowboys in an expert maneuver that doubled the cows back on themselves. Whooping it up, shooting their pistols, they got the herd milling, running around and around in a wide circle. Riders stayed on the outside of this melee of hoofs and horns as the mad steers with their lathered bodies and with heads down and tails up began slowing more and more.

For another hour the milling went on, until the cattle began to tire. They slowed to a trot, then to a walk, and finally the leaders put down their heads to hunt for grass tufts cut by the pounding hoofs.

The exhausted trail hands, cursing the stupidity of their charges, wiped caked mud and sweat from their faces and dug it from eyes, nostrils and hair. Panting horses, covered with white foam, hung their heads as they rested where they stood.

And as the exhausted cowmen began to take stock of the herd, and their own fatalities, the first gray streamers of the new day lightened the sky.

Two men who had left Rose Valley with such high hopes had died that night, one by the bullets of the attacking night marauders, the second cut to ribbons by the sharp hoofs of the cattle when his horse had broken a leg stepping into a treacherous hole. Another had taken a bullet through the hip. He was bandaged up, and started on his way back to Rose Valley, since he could not make the long trip to Kansas in such condition.

"We lost 'bout seventy head," Herb Malcom told the Rio Kid, as they drank hot coffee after a quick count.

"They're hightailin' it back to the valley, no doubt," Pryor agreed. "Let's not chase 'em. We got plenty of 'em left."

They let the herd graze until the sun was up, and then started on, crossing the river. About eleven A.M. they again paused permitting the cows to stop and rest until two o'clock, when the line of march was again resumed.

It was five o'clock when they reached the camping ground selected by the Rio Kid, once more out ahead of the herd.

"From now on," the Kid told Malcom, "we'll set a guard far enough out to give the alarm 'fore attackers git close enough to stampede us."

His army training made it possible for him to set sentries at strategic positions. They did this on each succeeding night, and as they moved the great herd slowly northeast toward Red River Crossing, over the vast Texas plateau, night after night passed without trouble, save for one occasion when one of the Kid's guards fired on an Indian who apparently had come to spy them out.

"Funny thing," the Rio Kid remarked to Malcom, whose face was grimly lined from the strain of the drive. "Those Indians back there that attacked us were ridin' shod hosses. So was this one that was spyin'."

"Mebbe they stole 'em from white men," suggested Malcom.

"Mebbe. But I heard one of 'em yelp durin' that fightin', and it didn't sound so much like Indian talk as it did a white man's cussin'."

"Dunno why any white men would attack us, Kid." Herb Malcom shrugged. "Still and all, they could, I reckon. I've heard tell of such. Mebbe they're outlaws, ridin' with Comanches."

The trail was taking its toll, however, a toll counted in the blood of the men who loyally stuck to their arduous job. But their one great compensation was that, under the leadership of Bob Pryor, the Rio Kid, the poverty-stricken men of Rose Valley were driving on to Kansas — on to wealth perhaps, or at least to a comfort that would be the salvation of the folks back home.

And one day the Rio Kid picked up Herb Malcom and pointed across the flats toward a rough shack which stood on the south bank of a wide river.

"That's the store at Red River Station, Herb!" he said jubilantly.

Herb Malcom stared at the goal toward which they had broken virgin trail with their herd. A hot sun beat upon them drying out the sweat of their bodies. Little cowbirds fluttered cheerily around the cattle now, chirping gutturally. Butterflies winged in the air, and the sky was deep-blue, with tiny puffs of white clouds crossing the dome.

"The Chisholm Trail starts across the river," the Kid told Malcom. "It's easy enough to follow to Abilene."

"Indian Territory," Malcom said slowly and thoughtfully staring out across the great wilderness.

"Yeah, but we'll go through," declared the Rio Kid.

"We'll go through," echoed Herb Malcom.

Since the night attack and the stampede, monotony had gripped the traildrivers. Each day was like the one that preceded it. Depression had gripped them as their spirits had fallen, though they bravely sought to conceal their feelings from one another. One and all they welcomed the diversion of the sight of a man-made building, no matter how rough and rude.

The store at Red River Station was run by a tough-hided pioneer. Like most of the frontier log houses it was looped for defense with holes through which to fire rifles to hold off Indian attacks.

The Rio Kid, scouting ahead of the herd to the river, was the first to reach it. He pushed Saber up to the building where several men lounged in the shade of the rough porch.

"Howdy!" sang out the Kid.

A couple of the men, one of them plainly the owner of the store, sat on boxes on the porch. A third man, tall and thin, leaned against a post on the far side. Facing the Rio Kid were two men whose looks he did not like. They were rough and tough, the type of men who wore their guns high and whose eyes were hard as they stared at Bob. That put Pryor on his mettle. He was too experienced at facing enemies, too expert at judging men at a glance, not to know what kind of men he was facing now.

The man slightly to the front as the Kid dismounted, stiff-legged, was a man of tremendous size, and heavy of body. Stringy black hair stuck out from under his Stetson, and he had a jutting, bearded chin and long bony legs. A tobacco cud bulged one leathery cheek, and as he masticated, his stained buck teeth showed behind his crooked lips. His hard black eyes were fixed upon Pryor calculatingly.

"How is it this gunny knows me?" the Kid asked himself. He could not remember ever having seen the big fellow before.

His swift glance took in the second man, a squat, wide rascal with straw-colored hair, a ragged, stained mustache of the same hue, cowlike brown eyes and a bulbous nose. At this worthy's belt hung a thick-handled bull-whip, the lash looped out of the way of his broad, mud-encrusted boots. He had on a blue woollen shirt, and wore leather leggings over his pants.

"Mule skinner," the Kid catalogued him.

Trailing Saber's reins on the ground the Rio Kid tried to step around the two who blocked the direct path to the steps. He was paying them little heed, his mind more on the fact that the warm air was filled with the sound of grunting pigs which dug in the dirt about the store, and with the homey cackle of chickens belonging to the trader who had set up at this spot to catch the new trail trade.

The big man did not give way, though.

He promptly moved so that Pryor bumped against him.

"Why, damn yore hide!" the gunny snarled. "Can't yuh walk without knockin' yore betters down?"

The Kid looked up into the man's ugly, whiskey-reddened eyes. "Honin' for a scrap, for some reason," he thought.

Aloud he said smoothly:

"Why, mebbe I was careless, Mister. Excuse me."

But as he tried to avoid the threatened brush, the big fellow seized his arm and whirled him around. Like a panther the Rio Kid whipped from his clutch, again facing him, this time with a calculating light in his strong eyes.

"Hands off!" he snapped, and this time he spoke with the Army officer's surety of being obeyed — spoke as to a subordinate.

The big man flushed and stuck out his chin.

"Slap him down, Tank!" advised the mule skinner from behind him. "Show him who's who in these parts."

So the squat man with the bullwhip was looking for trouble, too, was he?

For an instant the Kid stood, hands loose at his sides, not near his gun butts. He carried his guns Army style, butts reversed.

The short, broad fellow raised a paw, flecked with reddish hairs, to the handle of his whip. And in that instant the man he called Tank made a bad error by reaching for his Colt as he slapped at the Kid's face with his left hand.

Tank Loman's hard slap did not connect. The Kid skillfully seized the outstretched arm and jerked it, yanking Loman off balance with such surprising suddenness that the big fellow fell on his knees and hands in the yard dirt.

"Give it to him, Dog!" Loman cried, cursing furiously.

And "Dog" Donnolly, the mule skinner, drew his bullwhip and flicked back the lash.

Pryor knew the deadliness, at close range, of such whips. They could tear out a man's eye, ribbon his flesh. Tank Loman had come up on one knee, was again going for his gun. There was nothing for the Rio Kid to do now but make a fight for it. That was what they wanted.

The Kid's draw was lightning and his Colt boomed, echoed from the building. Dog Donnolly gasped a curse. His hand, clutching the whip, relaxed and the blacksnake fell to the ground.

A gush of blood came from the flesh of his forearm where the Kid's slug had drilled.

Whirling, Bob Pryor swung the Colt muzzle, pinning Tank Loman at half a dozen paces. Loman quit his attempt to get out his pistol. Fear yellowed his eyes as he gulped.

With every muscle of his lithe body ready for action, the Kid had his feet spread and his back to the porch as he faced his two hecklers.

From the dark interior of the store four men suddenly leaped out, guns drawn, covering the Rio Kid. They were obviously friends of Loman and Dog. Bob Pryor sighed. He was through unless he wanted to take the impossible chance of a scrap between two fires — and he was not ready to try suicide yet.

"Drop it and get up yore hands, hombre!" growled the leader of the gunmen quartet.

Slowly the Rio Kid began to lift his hand as his Colt clattered to the dust.

CHAPTER VI:
AMBUSH FOR EARP

"Ain't six to one sorta stretchin' it?" a deep voice drawled from the side of the porch.

Tank Loman had come up erect, his sneering lips twisted as he vented his fury against the Rio Kid, who had thrown him with a clever wrestler's trick, though he outweighed Pryor by fifty pounds.

The voice which spoke, chidingly, had a certain menacing, icy timbre to it which caused the half dozen gunnies, about to beat the Kid to the dirt and finish him, to freeze.

The square shouldered Pryor heaved an inward sigh of relief at the unexpected interruption. He glanced around and saw that the speaker was the tall, lean fellow who had been slouched at the other side of the store.

Pryor took a good look at him now. The young man had wide shoulders, a narrow waist, long arms and slim hands. Holsters attached to a cartridge belt rode at his middle, both empty. For the .45 Colts were gripped in his hand, the muzzles threateningly aimed at the murderous gang which had so wantonly picked a fight with Bob Pryor.

The Kid's new friend wore leather chaps, buckskin shirt, and Stetson hanging from the saddle on his waiting horse, standing at hand.

"Who the hell asked yore opinion?" snarled Tank Loman. "Shove those guns back and get goin', Mister, if yuh know what's good for yuh."

"I'm dealin' myself in on this," the deep, cold voice announced.

"Yuh'll be damn sorry for hornin' in like this on my bus'ness!" bellowed Loman. "Who in hell yuh think yuh are, anyhow?"

"My name's Earp, Wyatt Earp, in case yuh wanta find me agin sometime," the tall man drawled.

That name did not mean anything to the Rio Kid — then — any more than it did to the sneering tough who had heard it. But it was a name that was to become identified with the building of the old West, throughout the length and breadth of the wide land.

Young at that time, Wyatt Earp was just entering the full prime of manhood. He gave an impression of self-confident power, and

73

held himself with high dignity. One day, though he himself could not have guessed it then, he was to become one of the greatest of frontier marshals, always on the side of the right, ever against injustice and evil. Even at this age, in his early twenties, Earp had the aplomb of the man who has beaten the world and can take care of himself under any circumstances. Already, from the time he had been fifteen, Wyatt Earp had been driving stages and teams through hostile lands, had met and beaten the toughest gunmen the West had produced.

Earp was of the same timbre as the Rio Kid.

"Jest sift away from that there gent," drawled Earp, his gun steady as Fate. "Yuh can get goin', boys. We don't need yuh hereabouts no longer."

The Kid quickly drew out of the way, his gun rising to help Earp hold the toughs. With a furious curse, Tank Loman led the retreat to the bunch of horses waiting near at hand. The six mounted, Dog Donnolly gripping his punctured forearm, his mouth twisting evilly as he swore in pain and rage. Under the pistols of Wyatt Earp and the Rio Kid the half dozen mounted and rode east along the river bank, disappearing in the thick bushes and willows.

Pryor grinned, shrugging off the narrow escape with the insouciance of his daring nature. He swung around to thank the quiet, tall hombre who had horned in to save him.

"My name's Bob Pryor, mostly called the Rio Kid," he told Earp. "That was mighty fine of yuh, bustin' in for me like that. I'm scoutin' for a herd of cattle from Rose Valley, Texas."

The noncombatants on the porch were wiping sweat from their brows at the sudden cessation of the threatened gunfight. None of them had been pleased at the prospect of being such close eyewitnesses.

"Drinks're on me, boys," the storeowner announced. "I shore thought lead was gonna fly for a minute."

"I'm Wyatt Earp — yuh heard me say it," the lean fellow said to the Rio Kid quietly. "Wish yuh luck with yore cows on the Trail, Pryor. I'm huntin' buffalo in the Territory now, out from Abilene."

"Yuh got many men with yuh?" Pryor asked interestedly.

"Nope. Jest a good skinner. My idea is that a big party gets in each other's way and then they lose all their profits."

"Yuh've got plenty nerve," Pryor said admiringly. "Huntin' alone in the Nations, bangin' away at buffalo." He knew the dangers buffalo hunters ran, plying their trade in the wilds. The Indians objected to the slaughter of their food supply. There were thousands of redskins running loose from the Red to the Arkansas. Tough as the white hide hunters were, and as able to take care of themselves, many had been caught and scalped.

"We lost our flour, sugar and tobacco in a cloudburst — got washed into the river," explained Earp, as the young men strode inside the store together. "I done rode over here to pick up a new supply."

"That was shore lucky for me," the Rio Kid said, and smiled.

Wyatt Earp did not touch whiskey but accepted a glass of goat's milk, of which animals the storekeeper kept a small herd.

"Indians quiet?" asked the Kid, as they drank.

Earp shrugged. "Quiet as ever, I reckon. The Comanches raised hob last moon but I hear they've been drove back on their reservation by Custer's troopers. Yuh'll meet some thievin' beggars but likely not real trouble. There's another bunch of buffalo hunters west of my stand. Mebbe yuh'll run into 'em. Well, it's time I was ridin', Rio Kid. I'm packed and ready to go. So long and good luck."

He put out his hand, and the two men shook. Earp waved to the storeman and his friends, strolled out, mounted and trotted his horse toward the crossing.

The Rio Kid followed him out, staring at the Red River that separated Texas and the Nations. Across there lay the trail that had been beaten by old Jesse Chisholm from Kansas when he led several thousand Indians to the Government reservation picked for them.

Through virgin wilderness the old Cherokee halfbreed had cut the way to break that trail which was now being put to use by the white cattlemen of the South. It had been a back-breaking task to break that trail originally, the Rio Kid knew. He had heard many a tale of the hardships encountered, particularly of how, where quicksand had been found, old Jesse Chisholm would run a band of horses back and forth until the treacherous footing was packed safe for the passage of men and cattle.

Bob Pryor asked a question or two of the storekeeper, concerning the best way to cross with the Rose Valley herd. Then he mounted Saber and rode back to the point where he had left Malcom and the other Texans.

They were waiting for him on the slopes overlooking the broad river valley.

"We can cross the Red at dawn," the Kid told them.

He turned in his saddle, staring down at the Crossing, able to see over the Red from the high point he was on now. Down below the regular ford, in the water, he saw black specks — men swimming their horses across. He counted them. There were six.

"Huh," he muttered. "Now I wonder if they'd drygulch Earp 'cause he gave me a hand?"

"What's wrong, Kid?" asked Malcom.

"A bunch of sidewinders I bumped into are headin' across the Red, out of sight of the Station," explained the Kid. "I reckon they're on the trail of a friend of mine." Briefly he told Herb Malcom of the flare-up at the store.

"Tank Loman!" exclaimed Malcom, because the Rio Kid had remembered the names of his assailants and had repeated them. "Why, I know that snake, and Dog Donnolly, too! Loman's been around the valley some. He's a bad hombre — a hoss thief and gambler. He took a shot at me once, cut a groove in my leg and wounded my hoss when I got too close to him while he was changin' brands on some mustangs.

Donnolly used to freight from Austin to Arizony till he killed a man in a fight. The law wants him now."

Major Ike Young, formerly of Jeb Stuart's Confederate cavalry, was *segundo* to Herb Malcom, chosen because he had an older head on his shoulders and was more experienced than the other cowboys on the drive. He had offered to go with the herd to give them the benefit of his experience. Brawny, red of hair and face, the major was a strong man and an able leader.

Most of the two dozen trail drivers from Rose Valley were in their early twenties. There were the two Sellers boys, light-haired, rangy and strong; George Baylor, small but wiry, always smiling and ready to jest; the inevitable "Shorty" Jackson, taciturn, but loyal; Gus Snyder, handsome and dark of hair; Dave and Phil Potter, another brace of brothers; Turner, and Ellison, Thompson, Elder — all from famous Southern families of pioneer stock. Many of them, young as they were, had fought under the Stars and Bars, having enlisted at the ages of fourteen or fifteen as drummer boys.

All of them had hot fighting blood coursing in their veins. The Rio Kid knew he would need to restrain rather than encourage this proclivity — and he knew that each

79

man's one idea had been to go to the aid of Wyatt Earp, the moment it was suggested he might be in danger.

"When do we start?" drawled George Baylor.

The same thought had occurred to Captain Bob Pryor, though it was none of his intention to let all these men go on such a mission. But he meant to go himself. He could not let Tank Loman overtake and kill Wyatt Earp.

"Yuh can't all go," he announced. "Herb yuh come if yuh want to — and Baylor, Celestino, Ellison, Jim Sellers. That'll be enough. Saddle up and foller me now. Major Young'll take care of the herd while we're gone."

Faces fell among those left behind. A little excitement after the monotony of the cattle drive would have been welcome.

A few minutes later Pryor, with Mireles at his side, hit the trail for the crossing.

Over the Red in the Territory, they found the broad beaten track, hundreds of yards wide — the trail taken by the first herds to Kansas. Swift riding, with the Kid in the lead, his eyes watching the ground sign and rising now and again to glance ahead, brought them up the slope from the river bed into the wilderness.

The bush and trees were thick as walls, save for the Chisholm Trail itself. Here and there the cattle had passed round larger trees, leaving them standing in the middle of the wide way. Where the country allowed, the herds had spread out wider. Those cattlemen coming later were always hunting new grass for their stock.

At a boggy stretch, the Rio Kid, leaning from the dun's saddle, saw the fresh indentations made by the shod hoofs ahead. The prints were slowly filling with water, so he knew they were picking up on Tank Loman and his gunnies.

He came up on the top of a rise, reining in there to take in the sweep of wilderness ahead.

"There they are, Celestino," he said, raising his hand to point.

From this high eminence he could see Wyatt Earp riding at a slow trot to the north, skirting in and out of the trees and bush. A couple of hundred yards behind Earp, and to the west of the buffalo hunter's trail, were Loman with two gunnies, the squat Dog Donnolly having the other flank with the remaining pair of killers.

The trail swerved to the east to avoid a thick pine stand, and Loman was cutting across to intercept Wyatt and catch him in ambush.

The Kid urged Saber down the slope at full-tilt. Evidently unaware he was being dogged, Earp had not looked around. Stealthily Loman was getting into position for a deadly shot.

"Got to stop 'em!" muttered the Kid as the dun sped fleetly.

But his heart was in his mouth. Would he make it? For already Tank Loman was throwing up his rifle to take aim at Wyatt Earp. Bob Pryor yanked out his .45 Army Colt and began shooting rapidly. The range was too long for a pistol, but the explosions, however, did what the Kid had hoped. They warned Earp who immediately spurted off the trail into the bush. Loman's first slug whipped within inches of the tall buffalo hunter, but did not strike him.

A moment later and the Kid, with the wind whistling past his ears, the thud of Saber's hoofs under him, saw smoke come from Earp's position.

The Texans were pounding on after Bob Pryor. As Loman looked back over his brawny shoulder and saw them coming, they set up the shrill Rebel yell. Dog Donnolly swung in his saddle to check them. Guns began blaring from both sides.

"Knock 'em over!" yelled Pryor.

They were rapidly drawing up on the enemy. The Texans' bullets whistled around Loman and his henchmen. Wyatt Earp was forgotten as they saw the charging horsemen bearing down, but he could take care of himself now.

Tank Loman emptied his rifle at them. Jim Sellers let out a yelp as he felt the burn of a slug along his ribs, but he kept on riding, the blood staining his shirt. The Rio Kid heard the whistle of enemy lead, and one slug ventilated his Stetson. Saber, the dun, snorted and galloped full-tilt toward the banging pistols and Winchesters of the foe.

The half dozen gunnies did not wait to clash with the Rio Kid. They had had a taste of his gun prowess before. They swung their horses and hit the bush, disappearing as Bob Pryor swept in.

Shooting as they fled, the killers split and headed west away from the Texans. Wyatt Earp stepped out on the Trail, shouting to Bob Pryor. Turning Saber away from the enemy, who had taken to the tall timber and were running for it, the Rio Kid galloped up to the tall buffalo hunter.

"Thanks," Wyatt Earp said simply. "Reckon that squares the account, Pryor."

The Kid grinned. "Saw 'em crossin' the

Red on yore trail, Wyatt," was all he said.

"I was ridin' right careless, at that, I reckon," Wyatt Earp drawled. "If ever I bump into that Loman snake again I'll know what to do."

CHAPTER VII:
RED INFERNO

Nobody knew better than the Kid how difficult it would be to run down Tank Loman's gang in the thick, tangled bush. He knew he would lose a lot of men running up on gunmen in the woods, and so he called off the pursuit. The purpose of the expedition had been accomplished — saving Wyatt Earp from death.

Seeing the lone buffalo hunter started on his trip back to his wagons, and making sure that Tank Loman had retreated far to the west, the Rio Kid led his followers back to the cattle camp.

At dawn they started the herd toward the Red River.

The Kid was in front, the cattle strung out for over a mile behind him, guarded by point men, flankers, and the drag. In irregular formation, like scattered leaves blown across a field, the longhorned steers slowly approached the water. The van broke formation, lumbered down the bank, and trotted across a sand bar to the edge of the stream. Rains had swollen the Red, and it was filled with driftwood. Knee-deep, the cattle put down their muzzles to drink.

The Rio Kid, mounted on Saber, out in the water, picked a big steer from the van. He pushed Saber close and urged the longhorn out into the river. The huge brown body, horns held high, took the water, and Saber skillfully headed off any attempt at turning down river. Now the first steer was swimming, and a few others followed his lead. Malcom and his boys were working the leaders to the swim.

This was the danger point — establishing the line. There was always the danger that the leaders would turn downstream and split, with nervous animals behind shoving those ahead into a seething, murderous jam.

The skill of the Kid, Saber's aid, and the Texans' hard work, established the swimming line. With an inward sigh of relief, Pryor saw the leaders emerging dripping wet on the north shore of the Red River. He swam on across now, to unclog the landing point. Luck and skill had combined to prevent the cattle from milling in the center of the stream.

The hundreds on hundreds of cattle took

the water, the following longhorns docilely obeying the herd instinct and never breaking from the trail the leaders set.

Over in the Territory, the line of march was resumed. Once more Bob Pryor, the Rio Kid, rode far ahead to scout the trail. Point riders, flankers and drag men were in position as the meandering herd, stretching back into the dusty distance, lined out for Kansas.

Indian Territory, "the Nations," was mostly all unexplored wilderness of mountains, rivers and prairie, teeming with buffalo, other game, and hordes of troublesome redskins moved from the more populous East by the United States Army. In this vast unsurveyed space here and there was a dot of civilization's advance guard, a far-flung army post where a small detachment of cavalry was supposedly ready to police the wilds.

Actually there was little restraint. The Creeks, Comanches, Osages, Wichitas, Wacos, and half a dozen other tribes roamed the country at will. When they felt like it, the redskins would visit an Indian agent's store, and receive free food. At other times they went on the warpath, killing and looting, and at such times the army men had their hands full.

But the savage hordes were not the worst of those who made the Territory a danger zone for law-abiding white men. As soon as it was opened by the government the riff-raff of the Border had flocked to it, finding there a safe abiding place between their depredation sorties.

So it was that on the night that the Rose Valley herd, led by the Rio Kid, camped at the side of the Chisholm Trail which led to the great cattle market of Abiline, Kansas, a murderous gathering collected in the primeval wilderness. Red men were bent on being despoilers. But there was more evil brewing than that.

North of the Washita River and the mountains through which the stream ran, stood a great Indian village on the bank of a wide creek that fed into the Washita from the west. To the east not many miles off, ran the Chisholm Trail. Tepees formed of thick buffalo hides sewn together, and resting on long poles of mountain ash and other hard woods favored by the savages, stood thick along the bank of the creek.

Smoke rose from the outside cook fires that were red glows in the night. Mangy dogs bayed at the gibbous moon and, mingling with the odor of burned meat and hair was the clear, bracing odor of the west wind, bringing an aromatic aroma from the stands of huge pines and spruces on the mountainsides.

Women and children, talking in low, guttural tones, squatted outside the wigwams. Warriors sat in circles or stood guard over the great bands of hairy wild mustangs. Several buffalo carcasses, cut up for use as food, hung from crude cradles out of reach of dogs and marauding coyotes. A low humming sound, impossible to identify, sounded from the horde of savages, like the droning of myriad bees.

In a great tepee set apart from the main village squatted or lounged a dozen men. The flaps were drawn, but a small bowl of burning buffalo grease yielded a dim yellow light. The smell of it was choking and rancid, the interior of the tepee smoky, though much of the vapor was sucked up through the hole left at the top where the poles joined together.

A man with a heavy-set body occupied the center of this sinister gathering. His bear-like chest was painted with red and black stripes, and his brawny legs were encased in deerskin with fringes trimmed with blue and yellow beads. In a band about his jet-black hair were set curving buffalo horns, but he had removed the gargoyle mask of the medicine man and his own brown face was visible, showing his low, ferocious brow, his slitted eyes, and heavy lips. His skin was dark, but did not have the coppery tinge of most Indians, nor were the cheekbones as high as a pure-blooded savage's might be. The flat nose, the mixed color of the smoldering eyes, showed him to be a "breed," a cross between Indian and white man.

Virgil Colorado was his name, and he was the most powerful medicine man in the Territory. Facing him squatted a big man in buckskins and a beaver hat — a man whose face was twisted with rage. At one side lounged a large, bony fellow with a jutting chin, and at Virgil Colorado's other hand was a wide-bodied white man, with an untidy, straw-colored mustache and bulbous purple nose.

There were three more white men, hard-eyed, desperate devils whose guns showed that they had seen constant use. The rest of the assembly was made up of Indian chiefs who were ranged near Colorado, their stolid faces never changing as they listened to the talk, which they did not understand since it was in English.

The big man in the beaver hat spoke in a low voice that quivered with fury.

"I tell yuh they'll be near here on the Trail

within a few days, Colorado! Yore warriors can take 'em easy — there's only two dozen."

Virgil Colorado never smiled. His expression was characteristically lowering and sullen. He had a slow way of speaking, as though he weighed every word twice before allowing it to issue from his thick bluish lips.

"Don't forget, though, that the Texans are brave fighters and always good shots," he admonished. "Besides, the soldiers will hunt for us if we strike. Pahuska — Long Hair — whom you call Custer, beat the Indians on the Washita. Three Stars, too, the general called Crook, is none too far away."

"Yuh can kill them all!" argued the other. "Then how will they savvy where to find yuh or know who attacked 'em?"

Virgil Colorado shrugged his thick shoulders. The white blood in him made him more expensive than his Indian brothers. He was also more cunning in his mental processes. Despite their inherent savagery, pure-blooded Indians could never match the depths of evil that a twisted white brain could devise. Too, he had a clear knowledge of the value of money, and his eyes shone with cupidity as the tempter opposite him painted a picture of the profits to be made.

"There's forty thousand dollars worth of beef in that herd from Rose Valley, Colorado!" The man in the beaver hat pressed his point. "Tank and Dog here'll help yuh. So will my other men, and I'll be there myself. I have a feud of my own with one of them trail drivers — a hombre they call the Rio Kid."

Again the half-breed medicine man shrugged.

" 'Your feud is your pleasure'," he quoted an old Indian saying. "What I want to know is, if we attack these Texans, what is there in it for me?"

"Half what we sell the cattle for. Tank Loman's got connections in Abilene, and will handle the deal. And this will be jest the start. There'll be other herds comin' up the Chisholm Trail and we can work on the same basis. Yuh'll get rich!"

Virgil Colorado ruminated in the heavy silence that momentarily fell upon the gathering in the great tepee. Not far away a coyote bayed, a mournful sound in the wilderness, penetrating above the subdued hum of the Indian village.

At last the notorious breed spoke.

"I hate the drivers of cattle," he said sullenly. "I hate all men who invade our hunting grounds, killing buffalo. I hate the soldiers sent by the *wasichu*. I can foresee that the Indian will die with the buffalo. I, too, have a plan to stop such things, but I will not tell it to you now. But I need guns and bullets, with which to arm my men. Pahuska tries to keep those from us by every means. We have some, but we need more."

"I've brought one hundred new rifles with me," the big man said eagerly. "And pack mules, loaded with ammunition. I have men guarding them, a few miles from here. I brought them for you, Colorado."

Virgil Colorado's eyes gleamed. He turned and spoke to the chiefs beside him and they answered him in grunts. There was no way to tell, until the breed leader spoke again, whether the reply was favorable or not.

"Iron Hawk and Sitting Eagle," he finally informed in his ponderous, slow way, "say they will supply the warriors. They will be young men and reckless, under your command. But remember, once turned loose they will be hard to stop. The taste of blood inflames the panther. I will be there to watch but I will not take part unless you win."

"Then yuh'll take part," the man in the beaver hat declared grimly.

"As to the rifles," went on Virgil Colorado, "you will bring them to me here by tomorrow night."

He ended the interview with a wave of his stubby hand. The big man who had instigated the terrible plot rose, stretched his powerful muscles. His cronies followed suit.

"All right, then," he said. "Tomorrow we'll work out the details. I figger we'll let the Texans keep their steers till they're closer to market. That'll make it easier for us. Then we need to pick a spot where there'll be no chance of help comin' to 'em. We'll have to kill every one of the Texans. But remember — this Rio Kid belongs to Tank and me."

CHAPTER VIII:
SURPRISE ATTACK

Bob Pryor, the Rio Kid, scouted the way two miles out ahead of the point men of the Rose Valley herd, laboriously plodding on through Indian Territory toward the Kansas goal.

Behind them lay miles of trail, spelling days of sweat and strain, of dangers met and overcome. They had crossed the Red River, the Big and Little Washita, skirting the foothills of the Washita Mountains. At Turkey Creek and the North and South Canadian Rivers they had found trouble and excitement in working the great line of steers safely across the swirling waters.

Another puncher had been killed. He had been carried under the waters of the Canadian and drowned before he could be extricated from a milling ring of big animals. Every man among the drivers, from Herb Malcom to the youngest drag man had lost every ounce of fat on his body. They were men of muscle and bone, hard as iron, their faces grim, and determined to complete their task.

Now, in the west, rose blue-topped mountains. Ahead lay the Cimarron. The country was broken by great stretches of wooded areas, virgin timber untouched by man. Buffalo herds grazed beside the Chisholm Trail, the huge shaggy bulls raising their heads to stare at the rider on the dun, the advance guard of the oncoming men and cattle.

Before the rider stretched the endless billows of the land ocean; the prairies. The cattle drive had already crossed sections of flat, high-grassed ground, showing what was to come — and now came the prairies, beyond which lay their goal.

"We'll make it, Saber," the Rio Kid told the rangy dun.

His deep-blue eyes, with sun wrinkles at the corners, moved constantly as he rode. His keen gaze swept the terrain from ground to sky — watching the ground for sign such as hoof or foot mark, a newly overturned stone or freshly snapped twig; and the sky, where birds or the flash of sun on metal might give a warning. Smell, hearing, touch, sight, even taste were made use of by an expert scout; and a sixth sense which could only be called a developed instinct such as wild animals live by.

The afternoon was well along and it was time to pick a camping ground for the night. The Rio Kid sought such a spot now, where the Rose Valley steers might be held off the Trail — a place that would have grass and, if possible, water.

The Chisholm Trail here ran through a narrow, peaceful-looking valley. Cottonwoods and tremendous oaks with gnarled trunks and huge branches fought for the light with other growth. On the summits of the hills, east and west, the dark colors of spruce and pine showed, the western rim deeply shadowed as the sun fell behind the tops of the evergreens. Birds flitted across the Trail.

The Rio Kid could see that the valley narrowed at its northern extremity. The land was uneven, mostly hillocks covered with thick bush, while to the east showed jagged bare cliffs of red rock that caught the sunlight in a blood color.

His ears keened to every slightest sound, the Kid heard the first crackling of dry brush that broke the peaceful silence of the valley. Mingled with the noise of breaking limbs and brushing leaves was a thudding sound that Bob Pryor quickly identified as the beating of heavy hoofs on earth.

Saber, catching the scent from the west wind, sniffed, quivering a warning along his black stripe. The Rio Kid reined in the dun and drew back behind a pile of high rocks from which he could watch the Trail.

Presently a huge, shaggy buffalo bull with lowered head and small eyes gleaming in his immense skull, crashed through the bush onto the Trail from the west. At his hoofs thundered more of the animals, blindly dashing through the undergrowth. It was a small bunch of a hundred or so that had been grazing above. Alarmed by something, they had stampeded.

Pryor watched them as they charged over the Trail and broke into the woods at the eastern side.

For a time he sat Saber silently, slight corrugations between his slitted eyes. His hand sought the scar of the wound he had received at Gettysburg during the Civil War. The flesh had scarred for an area over his ribs, and the nerves there reacted differently from those in the uninjured tissue. It was uncanny how they twitched when subconsciously Captain Bob Pryor was aware of danger.

"Them buffalo shore weren't runnin' from us, Saber," he murmured, and waited, staring westward toward the pine forests on the slopes.

Nothing showed, however. If a band of Indians had been running the buffalo, to kill for meat, they would be galloping hot after them. Moreover, the big beasts were not easily stampeded.

Ears alert, the Rio Kid listened. Somewhere in back, buffalo hunters might have cornered some of the animals and started shooting them. But he heard no gun explosions, and could not have missed them, for the Sharps guns most of the hunters used sounded like small cannon.

Peace was again over the wilderness. But it did not return to the Rio Kid. A sign might mean nothing and it might mean everything. He could know no peace until he was certain that all was well.

He sat his saddle, observing the west slope as the sun slowly sank behind the ridges. The glory of the sunset blinded his vision to an extent, but he was able to note birds north and south of a certain section.

Already warned by the unexplained dash of the buffalo bunch, he checked this. Now and then a black speck — a crow — would approach the vacant sky space over a stand of great pines, and as suddenly dart off.

He looked south. A dust haze rose, for the Rose Valley herd was slowly approaching.

Herb Malcom was riding point, with Celestino Mireles on the other flank. They had their bandannas up around their mouths and nostrils to sift out some of the rising dirt that covered their clothing and gear in layers.

It was time to stop the cattle for the dark hours, to turn them into a circle and bed them down. The Rio Kid swung Saber and trotted back until Malcom could see him. He waved his hand, and Malcom gave the signal to the drivers behind him, each one relaying it to the next. The trail boss trotted his horse out to meet the Kid.

"Keep a tight watch, Herb," Pryor ordered. "I'll be back. Got to see to something while yuh bed down."

"Where you go, General?" called Celestino.

The Mexican lad had worked hard during the drive, but it was monotonous work. He was pining for excitement, and had an idea it was generally about in the Rio Kid's vicinity.

"I'm takin' a ride over yonder," replied the Kid, waving his arm toward the west. "You stay here. Be back in a little while."

With a sigh young Celestino Mireles nodded, as did Herb Malcom. They began to shove the leaders of the herd to the east, starting them in a slow circle, as the following bunches came up. It would take about an hour to bed the thousands down in the high grass off the Trail.

Bob Pryor rode Saber north, working close to the wall of bush so that he would be hidden from eyes on the ridges. He came to the freshly smashed trail that had been cut by the running buffalo, turned the dun into it, and began working west. The sun was still up, beyond the mountains, but its direct rays no longer struck the valley, save on the eastern summits.

A grateful shade had fallen over the great wilderness.

Pryor rode cautiously, knowing the dun would warn him of anything coming, if he failed to hear it himself. Saber had many keen instincts denied to man, and he was always on the alert for the scent of strange horses or humans.

For about a mile the land rose gently as the mouse-colored horse followed the back track of the buffalo band. Suddenly Saber slowed, his black stripe shivering the hide over his backbone. He gave a quick sniff which informed Pryor that the dun had caught the smell of something he did not like.

Without loss of a second, the Rio Kid

picked a spot where he could enter the bush and trees without disturbing a leaf or tree branch. He already knew that since he had been traveling on the beaten way the buffalo had come, that most of the dun's prints were not discernible.

He had hardly concealed Saber and himself among the trees when a tall young Indian brave came running from the west. The Indian's body was naked save for a loin cloth of hide about his middle. Fastened in the band holding his black hair were three eagle feathers, each indicating an enemy slain in battle. His high-cheek-boned face was painted with white and red clay streaks, and in one hand he carried a new rifle. A new cartridge belt holding shells for the gun was slung from a brawny shoulder.

"Now where'd he get that new pop-gun?" mused the Kid, his jaw tightening.

The brave's fierce black eyes darted from right to left as he kept sniffing the air like a hound on a rabbit's trail. The Kid held his left hand on the dun's warm neck to warn Saber to stand quiet. Saber was quivering. He hated the smell of the Indian and of the hairy little mustangs the savages rode, and which were now near. For on the heels of the red-skinned scout came half a dozen warriors, all armed with new rifles. They were afoot, but a hundred yards behind appeared mounted Indians, leading the bareback mustangs which were the mounts of their scouts up ahead.

The Rio Kid, peering through the interstices of bush, and as frozen-still as a statue, suddenly started. A giant chieftain, wearing buckskin pants, and with a full head-dress of eagle feathers showed among a bunch of passing savages. His face and breast were daubed with red and blue clay.

"That's the devil that attacked us in Texas!" the Kid muttered.

His gun hand itched. There was something so unusually sinister about the giant chief that Pryor's fighting blood boiled.

"Damn him!" he railed silently. "He's follered us all the way up the Trail!"

The chief passed on beyond the Kid's narrow range of vision. It was of necessity limited since he had to keep himself well hidden.

The Rio Kid counted about fifty Indians in the band as he waited for them all to pass. It was plain enough to the watching white scout that they had been lying hidden on the ridges, among the pines, waiting for the Rose Valley cattle drive to come in sight. It was they who had started the band of buffalo down, and the birds the Rio Kid had noted had been avoiding them.

He swung the dun away from the hot deer trail he had followed, hustling for the cattle camp. With all speed the drivers must be warned of the sinister war party in the neighborhood. As he came nearer to the Chisholm Trail, he cut south into the brush, so as to work around past the spot where he calculated the savages must be hiding, waiting for night. Rarely would any Indians attack except at night, in the moonlight. They did not often take the risks of a frontal attack on armed whites.

It took Bob Pryor time to make his way quietly through the woods and avoid being seen, but he made all haste possible. Darkness was close at hand; the air was already cooling. Even from the distance he could see that a cook fire had been built at the cow camp, and the herd had been stopped for the night, while weary drivers lounged about to rest.

He was within sight of the camp, hurrying to his friends, when he heard the pounding of hoofs to the west. A mass of Indians, mounted on mustangs, came charging in from his right, traveling at full tilt. They were upon him, cutting him off from his friends, before he could swing his mount.

The Rio Kid's Colt whipped out. His

shot, sent at the chief who was in the lead, knocked the Indian chieftain from his painted horse before the savage could pull the trigger of the rifle he was lifting. There were at least two hundred painted warriors in this bunch, the Kid coolly estimated, as he whirled Saber to escape the fusilade of deadly bullets from their guns.

Discovered, the Indians set up a whooping, their war cries ringing all through the valley. The Kid cut down for the main Trail trying to keep a shelter of trees between himself and the savages.

Deafened by the yells and shooting of the new bunch he nearly ran into the guns of the first group he had spied, who now were coming on with a rush toward the cattle camp.

CHAPTER IX:
MASSACRE

Going at full tilt as he swept out onto the wide swathe of the Trail, the Rio Kid saw the big chief once more on his little mustang, coming hell-for-leather, bunched with his riders. Screeches rose as they spied the Rio Kid, and pistols were hastily flung up for aim. The Kid drove a spur into Saber's flank, even as he emptied his first Colt at random into the oncoming wave of savages. An Indian crashed as his horse went down. Two more, following, piled up on him, forcing the others to swerve.

Whipping a second gun from his holster, the Rio Kid fired again and again as the dun, picking up speed, flying like the wind, and uncannily zigzagging to escape the wild barrage of shots, galloped across the open area and hit the eastern bush.

As he gained the fringe of bushes, Saber leaped madly, high into the air. For a moment the Kid thought that the animal which was companion and friend to him had received a fatal dose of lead. But the big dun steadied, although blood flowed from the crease along his grayish hide. For two pins Saber would have turned and charged those firing Indians, loving a fight the way he did, but the Kid urged him on to a point of comparative safety where they would not be riddled.

"Yuh'll get plenty of scrap, boy," the Kid muttered tightly, between his almost continuous shots at the hardriding Indians.

He was trying for the big chief again, but by now the feather-decorated warrior was protected by the bodies of other Indians who rode in close to him. Half a dozen of the whooping, fighting redmen turned off the Trail after the Rio Kid. The rest charged straight on for Herb Malcom's camp, menacing shadows in the dimming light which in minutes more now would give way to black darkness.

Savage yells from the western side told Pryor that the larger bunch of Indians had come up from that direction and were attacking. Guns began to boom — the sharp crackle of the rifles of the trail drivers, hurriedly beginning their defense.

Blood flowed down the Kid's thigh, for the slug which had nicked Saber had also

107

cut a gash in Pryor's upper leg. He was too busy to notice a small thing like that, though, as the guns in his skilled hands picked off the leading Indian of the gang which had followed him.

Bullets smashed into the tree trunks, clipped the bushes about him, as he kept constantly shifting position to spoil the aim of his attackers. Saber would steady whenever he could, to give the Kid a fair shot.

The shooting from the cow camp was desperately fast and grew to deafening proportions.

"General! General!"

That was the voice of Celestino Mireles, calling to the man he had chosen to follow to the end. There was a note of agony in the young Mexican's cry.

"He's hit!" flashed to the Rio Kid's mind, as he saw red.

Cold fury surged through him, though his fighting blood rose to the boiling point. His accurate gun knocked a second Indian off his mustang, then suddenly he whirled Saber.

"Go get 'em, boy!" he snarled.

The surprise of his attack broke the ranks of the four savages bent on settling with this white scout. They shot hastily, their bullets singing about Pryor, but doing little damage beyond cutting a chunk from his strapped Stetson.

Colt blaring, the Kid shot down another naked red man, then Saber was on them, rolling the Indian ponies back with lashing forehoofs and snapping teeth, ruining the aim of the raiders. The Rio Kid put a bullet through the brain of one big warrior at two yards, blowing half his head off. Saber had knocked a mustang off balance, and as the animal rolled the rider sprang nimbly off, but the dun's hoof struck his head, cracking it open.

"We're through 'em!" shouted the Kid, twisting in his saddle to take care of the remaining pair.

He got one, and the other galloped off into the trees, whooping shrilly.

Pryor swung the dun to the Trail, riding for the cow camp like a madman as night fell over the awful scene. It seemed alive with Indians, some mounted, some on foot. The cook fire blazed red in the darkness, making eerie ruby shadows that flickered over the murderous fight. The onslaught had been so sudden, so brutal, that the cattle drivers had had but a few seconds in which to snatch up their guns and throw themselves down behind makeshift cover. The biggest surprise had been that, unlike most Indians, these had attacked frontally.

As the Rio Kid charged in, the flash of rifles and bang of Colt revolvers made it difficult to hear. In the glow the Rio Kid saw the brutal faces of Indians leaping in, shooting as they came as Malcom's Texans tried bravely to fight back. The camp was entirely surrounded, and to the south the cattle herd, alarmed by the guns, was stirring, starting to pick up speed and run down the valley.

"Celestino!" roared Pryor, his voice rising above the battle tumult. "Malcom! Grab yore hosses! Ride!"

But even as he yelled, a groan followed his words.

They were caught! It was too late to mount. Indians were already among the horses, were running them off.

On the other side of the camping ground, Pryor caught sight of the big chieftain, leading the attack. He fired, but the range was difficult, and Indians were turning on him the instant he charged.

Shrieks and whoops mingled with the roar of gunfire. The Kid, driving Saber at full-tilt, galloped around the dark outskirts of the melee, sending in killing slugs where they would do the most good. As he came to the eastern side, against the fire glow he saw a tall young brave seize Gus Snyder, from Rose Valley and, with a razor-sharp knife, rip off the dying young white man's scalp, waving it high as the blood spattered on the earth and over the victor's naked body.

The Potter brothers were fighting side by side. Dave Potter took a slug through the lungs and his brother Phil sprang forward to lift him. Half a dozen Indians leaped upon them, shooting, slashing.

Shorty Jackson was stretched out on the ground, dead, his smoking rifle still clutched in his hand. Major Turner, crouched back of a rock, was still shooting, but as the Kid tried to drive in to help him, a wave of Indians came up behind the old man. The Kid got three before the others rolled on, leaving the horribly mutilated major behind them.

"No quarter, no mercy!" howled the Kid, his heart one stabbing ache of pain and hatred. He had seen men die like flies in the Civil War, but this —

His quick eye sought Herb Malcom in the carnage, but the trail boss was nowhere in sight, either alive or dead. And then he saw Celestino Mireles, the boy who was even more to him than a younger brother, the youth whose protector the Rio Kid had

111

become.

With his Mexican sombrero hanging by its leather strap down his back, Celestino was staggering from the ring of light toward the man on the dun horse. His arms were outstretched to the Rio Kid in supplication. Blood covered his young face, and his gritted teeth gleamed in the fire glow. He was badly wounded, hardly able to walk, but still he was trying to reach the man who was his one friend in the world.

Even as the Kid leaped Saber toward Celestino, an Indian brave sprang from behind a tree, knife raised to deal young Mireles a finishing blow. But the Rio Kid's Colt was quicker. His slug caught the Indian between the shoulder blades, to tumble him dead at Celestino's feet.

"Celestino — this way!" shouted the Kid.

Mounted savages were after him, shooting, screeching their hatred at this elusive enemy who had dealt them such hard blows — an enemy who seemed to weave in and out among them ghostlike, dealing death on every hand.

Two pushed their mustangs toward him, from opposite sides. He shot one through the nose as he felt the sting of the second red man's slug on his own cheek. He swung on the shooting Indian, with a quickly shouted order to Saber.

Sweat and blood soaked the raging Kid, foam covered the hard-battling dun as Saber reared, forehoof's plumping into the barrel ribs of the Indian mount. As the jolt loosed the savage's knees the Rio Kid got him with a shot that knocked him clean from his seat. A quick hand caught the rope halter of the mustang before the hairy little chestnut recovered balance, and the Kid shoved in.

"General, my General!" Celestino gasped. "They have us!"

The Rio Kid reached down, scooped the slim lad up and, turning, spurred Saber into the darkness, carrying the boy in his arms and leading the Indian's mustang with a jerk. Young Mireles was trembling violently, evidently badly hit.

There was nothing more that could be done for the handful of Texans now. The few who were alive were fast dying. And even as Bob Pryor fought his way through, lithe red bodies swept over the camp like a bloody tidal wave, engulfing those pioneer drivers of the Chisholm Trail.

Pryor glanced back, wiping sweat from his burning eyes as Saber tore on as though his hoofs had wings. The mustang raced to keep up, as if madly running away. There was no more shooting now, but blood-thirsty, yelling savages were bending over bodies, plying their scalping knives. The ruby fire glow flickered over a scene of carnage and brutal death too horrible for contemplation.

A tall, painted savage, with an eagle feather stuck in a headband, working around toward the spot where the Rio Kid had been striking their flank, suddenly rose up in his saddle.

"Hey, Chief!" he screamed in English. "There he goes! The Rio Kid! After him, boys!"

Not too far distant to hear, prickles ran up and down the spine of the Rio Kid as the full meaning of those words slapped him in the face.

"That's no Indian!" he growled in his throat, his lips tight and set. "And I've heard that voice before!"

But, above all else, the most important thing now was to get Celestino out of danger.

"Can yuh hold to a hoss?" he said in the lad's ear.

Young Mireles was gasping, and blood welled from his side. His clothing was sopped with the crimson flood.

"Pairhaps, pairhaps," he said very bravely, trying to keep his lips from trembling. "Eet hurts *mucho,* General!"

The giant Indian chief, warned by the cry of the disguised white man, was already waving his arms, yelling at some of his followers, organizing pursuit after the Kid. Pryor knew he had not a moment to lose, Saber's stout heart would carry on for a time, but he could not carry double at high speed for many miles.

He urged the dun east into thick bush, as pursuit began, in his mind and soul bitter tumult — and one fixed, firm determination. These devils *must* not — *should* not — get him! Not that he valued his own life so highly, but the Rio Kid must live — for revenge.

Indians were following up the great cattle herd which had stampeded south on the back-trail, only a cloud of dust being left to show where the hope of the Rose Valley folks had bedded down. The attackers had run off the remuda of horses, and others were busy robbing the sprawled, mutilated corpses.

Thirty mounted men started from the camp site on the Rio Kid's trail. Out in the darkness he hit the ground and swiftly set Celestino in Saber's saddle where he could be tied, for the Indian mustang had no saddle; only a blanket, fastened about his hairy ribs. With his rawhide lariat, Pryor tied young Mireles to Saber's saddle, whispering a cautioning word in the dun's velvet ear.

"Easy, now, Saber," he warned. "No buckin', no monkey-shines, savvy?"

The dun sniffed, nuzzled at his master's cheek.

"Hold on, Celestino," the Kid commanded.

He drew in the rope fastened to the Indian horse's halter, and sprang up, mounted bareback. Celestino slumped over in Saber's leather, holding to the horn. Born to the saddle, the Mexican youth would keep his knee grip as long as any consciousness remained and then the Kid counted on the ropes.

They were hunting for the Kid in the night, spread out, beating the black thickets. He heard them coming closer as, leading Saber, he headed for the tall timber on the eastern slopes of the valley. Bullets, blind in the dark, hunted him, too. But he did not reply, for he had no intention of giving away his position.

Alone he could have faded away, escaped. But for nothing on earth would he have deserted the wounded Mexican lad.

As the bloody miasma of the battle that had clouded his brain cleared somewhat, the Rio Kid found that his chief emotions were overwhelming fury against those who had so horribly massacred the Texans, and self-accusation that ate into his soul.

"I led 'em here, and I'm the one advised 'em to drive their cows to Kansas," he accused himself bitterly.

Yet such an overwhelming attack as that was unusual, and could not possibly have been foreseen, or guarded against. There had been no news of tribes on the warpath when the Kid had come south on the Chisholm Trail, before meeting with the Rose Valley pioneers.

"And I can make a damn good guess who that tall jigger fixed up like an Indian is!" he muttered aloud. "I wouldn't forget that voice. Tank Loman!"

Suspicion burned in his brain. Loman evidently was in cahoots with the savages, probably had led them against the Texans, and if that were the case, what other white men who took the trail might be due to face was too horrible to think about. In a way, what had just occurred explained some of Loman's other activities though.

"Figger he's a lookout for the Indians," the Kid decided. "To let 'em know when a cattle drive's comin' through."

CHAPTER X:
RUNNING FIGHT

Rising lazily from behind the black velvet horizon, the moon was sending a silvery glow over the world, except where trees and bushes cast dense shadows. In a shaft of moonlight the Kid, in glancing back, saw the pain-racked face of the young Mexican whose curved lips and aquiline nose were drawn up in agony.

This eager youth, whose family had been murdered on the Rio Grande by the same gang of red raiders who had finished Pryor's own parents and devastated the Border, was the only human being the Rio Kid could call his own. The lad had attached himself to the youthful Pryor, giving a hero-worship that a younger brother offers an elder — and Bob Pryor could not have loved him more had he been blood kin.

Obviously Celestino was losing his strength, still bleeding.

"Have to stop soon as I dare," decided

Pryor, "and see what I can do."

For the first time he took stock of his own condition. Burning and stinging sensations came from his thigh, where a jagged flesh wound had clotted. He had a singe along his bronzed cheek which stung annoyingly, and another chunk of skin had been torn off his upper left arm. Bullets had riddled his clothing and his Stetson. Garb and body were caked with blood, sweat and dust, and his throat was as dry as an old leather boot.

As he steadily drove the Indian mustang through thick bush, he came to the winding stream which cut this valley. It was not more than a few yards wide, meandering through the wilderness. There was the chance that its bed might be quicksand, but the Rio Kid, getting his second wind as he scooped up a Stetson full of water and drank, while the horses sank their muzzles deep into the cool fluid, decided he had to take a chance.

"The only way," he muttered, as he brought Saber's head up so that he could press a drink on Celestino. The lad was weakening by the moment, losing more and more blood.

"They'll hunt us the way they saw us run, for awhile," he figured, listening intently for sounds of his pursuers.

He heard them, heard the crackle of bush,

the thud of hoofs. Then a low cry as one searcher called to another. Where the growth was thick these expert trackers could follow even in the darkness, follow by the broken trail of bent branches and disturbed leaves.

Hastily he got the horses into the bed of the stream, letting them pick their footing. It was the only way he could cover trail.

"Figger they'll cross and head east, for awhile, anyways," he thought hopefully, for it was hardly likely the Indians would figure on their quarry following the stream.

A mile down the stream he drew up on the bank and dismounted. Celestino had lost consciousness. He was a limp bundle in the Rio Kid's arms when he was lifted from Saber's back.

The Kid cut away the wet, torn clothing over the wound, which was jagged and deep, and heaved a sigh of relief as he found, after close inspection, that the bullet must have hit a rib and been deflected, emerging instead of driving into the lad's vitals. The bleeding was the worst aspect, he decided, and he set about stopping that by applications of cold water. In the Civil War he had learned how to treat gunshot wounds.

With Celestino attended to he quickly washed his own hurts, binding them with strips of shirt.

Tying the lad again on Saber, he mounted the mustang and proceeded, trying to figure what the foes' moves would be.

"They'll hustle men up on the east rim," he mused, "to cut us off, that bein' the way it would look like we'd go. They've got the south trail blocked, and the north exit to this valley is narrow enough to be watched by a handful of 'em. They got their camp over there likely, seein' they come in from the west."

Lips grim, the Rio Kid deliberately swung westward. It was the one direction which seemed hopeless, for it would lead into deeper and deeper wilderness and the strongholds of the Indian tribes of the Nations. But his hope was that the enemy would not believe him foolish enough to go that way and if he was successful, he could get away by taking to the mountains.

Coming up to the Chisholm Trail, the Rio Kid's eyes and ears were alert. He could hear the Indians to the right, toward the camp site, and to the left the lowing of cattle told where they were holding the big herd, having stopped the stampede. The immediate space was clear, and within a half minute the Rio Kid had crossed it and plunged into the chaparral.

He shoved on and on, letting the Indian

pony pick the easiest footing as they mounted toward the western hills. He was too experienced to believe, however, that once out of the valley of death, he was safe from pursuit. Indians would soon pick up the sign, figure out his foxlike doubling trick, and start on his trail.

But he rode on, climbing to the western summits. Behind him lay the valley where a white mist rose from over the little stream. He was in wilderness — a strange country with nothing to follow but animal trails, used by the Indians.

Dawn found the Rio Kid still going, up and down through virgin territory. He was nearing the end of his own tether, and a look at the white, drawn face of Celestino Mireles told him that the lad must have some rest. The horses, too, were worn out.

Beside a little rill he made a quick camp. They could at least eat, for he had hardtack and jerked meat in Saber's saddle-bags. He took off the dun's saddle, and let Saber roll in the high grass. The Indian mustang he rubbed down, but kept him fastened on a rope stake.

The Kid tended Celestino. The weak youngster opened his eyes, to stare up into his friend's eyes.

"General — you should leave me," he

whispered. "Es-cape, yourself —"

"Quit talkin' nonsense," ordered Pryor, smiling. "Yuh must be delirious."

"Zey — zey keel all our frien's?"

"Afraid so."

"*Si,* ees so. I saw Senor Malcom die. He was theenkin' firs' of the cattle, leap' on hees horse to ride and stop zem."

"Yeah, he would. Figgered it was jest a passel of rascals come to stampede the hosses, I s'pose. Yuh say yuh seen him git it?"

Celestino nodded. "Zat beeg Indian chief, he fire at heem, and Senor Malcom sank on hees horse, ze horse run on but Malcom was dead, *si.*"

"Quit talkin' now and save yore strength," the Kid advised gently. "We got to snatch a few winks, and then we can go on. Make better time in the long run."

Saber would, with his keen animal senses, keep watch over them as they napped. Pryor was asleep instantly, head on his saddle, gun by his hand. . . .

Saber woke him, nuzzling at his cheek. The Rio Kid was instantly alert, gun in grip, ready to fight. The sun was well up in the intense blue of the sky and Pryor, staring back at the summits of the hills he had crossed, saw black specks winging to north and south — birds leaving the path of his pursuers.

"They're comin'!" he muttered.

He shrugged but quickly saddled up, fastened Celestino Mireles on Saber, mounted the mustang and swung on west. From a high point a backward glance caught the scintillation of sun on metal as the light struck a gun barrel.

Directly ahead a flock of crows set up a raucous cawing, flying swiftly off in alarm. The Indians would see them but it could not be helped. They had found the trail he had made as he had run through the wilds.

Forced to guess a route, not sure of what contours of rock and cliffs might block him, Pryor knew he was losing distance to the swift savages who were hot on the blood trail. Probably it would not be long now before he was forced to make a last stand. But the Kid meant to find a rock stronghold where he could hold them off until his ammunition ran out.

He forced the pace but it was slow going in spots. He could tell from backward glances that the Indian pursuers were picking up on him. He checked his guns for the final battle — the two Colts in the holsters, those under his armpits, his carbine.

Hardened to peril, the Rio Kid regretted

only that he could not live for revenge — revenge on the white men who, he was certain from what he had observed, had egged the Indians on to the ruin of the Rose Valley people.

"And them folks'll be waitin' back there in Rose Valley full of hope," he groaned.

That was his only concern. No fear for himself was in his make-up. He was too used to the expectation of violent, sudden death.

Crossing a bare space, he glanced back, saw a puff of smoke, and then heard a bullet strike into the rocky earth yards behind him.

"Sighted us!" he growled.

Back on the other slope he saw horsemen emerge from the bush, naked savages on their mustangs, eagerly on his trail.

"Mebbe this'll be the best place," he thought, seeing the jagged red rocks close at hand which would afford shelter for a time.

As he was heading toward the nest of rocks, however, to take his last stand, from the southwest he heard a heavy *boom* that echoed back and forth before dying away. It was followed by a second, and a third; steady, spaced firing of a big rifle.

"Buffalo gun," he said aloud. A faint tinge of hope came to him. "We won't stop yet," he decided.

Celestino sagged lower in Saber's saddle, holding to the horn, but with the elasticity of youth fighting for a new grip on life.

The Rio Kid pushed the mustang down the rocky slope, sliding in steep places, until he reached the bottom. Bullets spat from the place he had been shortly before. The Indians were coming on swiftly now, taking pot shots at him with rifles as they yelled and whooped triumphantly.

The heavy gunfire from the buffalo gun ahead grew louder as he rounded the hill and bore at an angle away from the dip.

Then, ahead, the Rio Kid saw a wagon with a canvas top. Near at hand was another, and a man was squatting beside the carcass of a huge buffalo, busy with a skinning knife. It was a white man, a skinner, busy while the marksman with the booming buffalo gun shot down the big game.

The skinner was a red-faced, carrot-topped man, burly and stubby, with a week-old beard, wearing a battered felt hat, a blue shirt, and leather pants over his corduroys which were tucked into black halfboots. Sweat poured down his flat-nosed, broad face.

The sight of Bob Pryor with his bloody bandages, and of the collapsed Celestino, galvanized him to action. He sprang up with a gruff oath, yanked his six-shooter and fired three quick ones into the air.

"What the hell!" he shouted. "You — you a white man?"

He stood there undecided for a moment, gun ready.

"We're huntin' help," the Kid called. "Watch yoreself! Indians a-comin'!"

A saddle horse stood tied to the wagon wheel. The red-haired man leaped over, snatched up a rifle, and hit leather, galloping west.

"Hey, Wyatt!" he shouted. "Injuns! Injuns!"

With the hot breath of the enemy on his neck, the Rio Kid followed after him. Already the van of the pursuit was in plain sight, shooting furiously. Gripping the body of the mustang with his legs he fired back, but the hairy little half wild horse did not like shooting from his back, and fought his rider. The Kid shoved on after the redhead, battling the fighting mustang, and not for an instant dropping the reins by which he led Saber.

The buffalo gun had stopped its steady booming, and the Kid rode on behind the red-headed buffalo skinner, towing Celestino on Saber, to where a tall man squatted. The heavy gun with which he had been picking off buffalo ranged in the draw before him was on a wooden rest, and his horse was close at hand.

"Earp!" cried the Rio Kid.

Wyatt Earp rose coolly and strolled over. His light-blue eyes fixed Pryor, and for a moment he did not recognize the Rio Kid, bedraggled as he was from the awful night fight and the run. Then he grinned and nodded.

"Hello, Kid," he drawled. "Yuh seem in a hurry."

The Kid's white teeth showed in a grin.

"You'd be, too, if yuh had my reasons — two hundred red devils on my sign!"

"Ride on west — yuh'll see my trail thataway," Earp said rapidly, as he rammed fresh shells into the revolving chambers of his Colt buffalo gun.

That gun shot a long .50-caliber slug, half an inch of leaden death that could stop a huge bull in its track. Such a bullet, hitting a man, would knock him head over heels. A "new-fangled" weapon at that time, it used the recently invented percussion shells in a revolving cylinder which had five compartments.

"C'mon, Red!" Earp said sharply. "Get yore rifle ready and we'll hold 'em up!"

"S'pose Red takes the boy on," suggested Pryor, "and I'll stick here with you, Earp."

Wyatt Earp shrugged his lean, broad shoulders.

"All right," he said dryly. "I don't reckon Red'll object much."

Earp swung a long leg over the saddle on his fast black.

"There's a deserted hunters' hut about half a mile from here," he told the Rio Kid, as he threw up his heavy rifle and took aim. "Reckon we can make that and hold out awhile. I got a cache of food in there, jest in case."

Rapidly the skinner called Red, leading Saber with Celestino on his back, disappeared around the draw where the dead buffalo lay. The Kid and Wyatt Earp opened fire on the Indians scuttling from the bushes to the east. Earp's first shot knocked one off his mustang, and the Rio Kid's accurate carbine took a second.

The deadly precision with which the two white men shot, cool and unhurried, appalled the growing horde. Two more took lead, and a horse crashed, screaming, its rider leaping to the dirt only to be knocked dead by Wyatt Earp's next slug.

"We better draw back a ways," Earp advised. "They're bunchin' up on us, Kid."

Chapter XI:
Guns of the Buffalo Men

Hot on Red's trail, the horses of Earp and the Rio Kid galloped westward. The growing band of savages whooped in eager anticipation as they surged forward, flogging their mustangs on.

Behind a clump of gray rocks, the Rio Kid and Wyatt Earp made another short stand, picking off the leaders of the war party, piling them up for a time until they began to flow to the sides in an attempt to flank the two whites. Then the pair moved swiftly on as bullets ripped the leaves, spat into the ground, and whistled about their heads.

"There he is!" Pryor snarled suddenly.

"Who?" asked Earp, over the crackle of enemy guns. Even in this stress there was a note of surprise in his voice. How was one murderous savage different from another?

"That big Indian — see him — the one with the eagle-feather head-dress!" snapped the Rio Kid. "He's follered us up from

130

Texas, damn his hide! And Tank Loman's in on this, too! He was with the redskins that hit us on the Trail and massacred my friends, stole their cattle!"

The tall Earp, unrattled in the face of what seemed sure death, was a fit fighting mate for Bob Pryor, the Rio Kid. Both were deadly shots with rifle and pistol, and both had cold-steel nerves that never betrayed them in excitement by tensing their muscles to spoil aim, or heating brains so that clear thought was impossible. Different in temperament and in physical aspect — for the Kid was jauntier and not so large as Earp, being the perfect weight and size for the ideal cavalryman — yet they matched each other in fighting ability. Each man was worth his weight in wildcats.

"There's the cabin," announced Earp, as they rounded a sharp bend.

The Indian mustang under the Rio Kid suddenly bounded high into the air. His head went down between his forelegs, and the Kid was forced to leap for his life. A bullet had killed the mustang instantly.

He saw the cabin then, about two hundred yards off, a roughly built shelter made of thick pine logs, and loopholed with slits which also served to let in whatever light entered the shack, for there were no win-

131

dows. It stood on a rise and the bush had been cleared for some distance around it. The door stood ajar, and Red was yelling for them to hurry.

"C'mon, c'mon!" he shrieked. "I wanta get this door shut, Wyatt!"

A ghost of a smile touched the wide, grim lips under the tawny mustache.

"Red's gettin' excited," Earp remarked, as he gave the Kid a hand to jump up behind him.

Earp fired a last shot as they headed for the hut. Saber whinnied the moment he saw the Kid, and started to run to him. An Indian Bullet sped past him, but found the heard of Red's mount, near the cabin.

"Back, run, Saber!" shouted Pryor.

Saber hesitated, then trotted off among the trees.

As the two men leaped down from the black, Earp slapped the animal's rump, starting him off to cover. They jumped inside the cabin and Red, sweat pouring down his lobster face, slammed the thick-slabbed portal and dropped the wooden bar into its slots.

"Phew!" he growled, glaring at the Rio Kid. "I ain't got nothin' against yuh, hombre, but yuh shore got an unpleasant swarm of hornets follerin' yuh."

"Take the west side, Red!" Earp commanded. "I'll take the south. You handle the east, Kid. If they git too thick on the north, we can jump over and clear 'em there."

Celestino Mireles came up on his knees, biting his lip.

"General — queeck! I weel reload. I can do eet."

Wyatt Earp was already shooting through one of the gun-slits. Outside, this slit was about a foot high and just wide enough for a rifle barrel to stick through; inside it widened so that the marksman could turn his rifle and command the space up under the wall, and could also see out without putting his eye directly to the slit.

"That's one," Earp remarked, as his heavy gun made the little cabin reverberate with its deafening repercussion.

The Rio Kid's carbine gave off a lighter note, but did its deadly work. Red was banging away as Indians filtered around to the far side.

Peeking from his slit the Rio Kid saw that already bodies of the enemy lay on the open ground around the shack. He took aim and picked a young painted savage off his mustang. The Indians, never liking frontal attack against such marksmen, turned their horses and faded back into the woods, dismounting and forming a circle about the hut.

"They got us," Red growled, drawing a deep breath. "We can't hold out in here forever, Wyatt."

"It ain't bad, Red," Earp told him banteringly. To the Kid he drawled, "Don't mind Red. He always sees the gloomy side of things, Kid."

Celestino was shoving fresh shells into spare guns removed from the hole hidden in the dirt floor.

"Lucky I filled the water barrel yesterday," Earp remarked.

The besiegers were shooting from the woods, hoping for a lucky shot through the narrow slits, but the bullets only pinged into the thick logs.

"Save yore shells," ordered Pryor. "Wait'll they charge."

More and more Indians were arriving each moment. Savage cries accented the bullets that were hurled at the quartet inside the hut, who made no attempt at long-distance shooting. They could hold out while daylight prevented the enemy from getting near.

Hours dragged out interminably. Once, in the afternoon, the Indians again tried a frontal attack, but quickly melted back among the trees under the terrible raking fire of the Rio Kid and Wyatt Earp.

In the lulls, the Kid and Celestino took naps, to gather strength for what would come in the night.

"They'll burn us out easy, when it's dark, Wyatt," Red Harper said glumly.

But despite his carping, Harper was a brave man. Older than Earp or the Kid, he weighed the possibilities of escape and, finding none, was hinting for suggestions.

Earp glanced at Pryor, then at Celestino. It was plain what he was thinking. With the Rio Kid's Saber and Earp's black the only horses available, they could not make any time even if they got out of the trap and could reach the two horses.

Night came down with a sudden swoop. Inside the cabin, ears were strained for the sounds of the Indians creeping in. The moon had not yet risen over the tops of the giant trees, so they could not see, but the ears of the men inside the hut were hypersensitive to catch the stealthy padding of bare feet on the earth, the faint rustling of grass, the movement of a stone; any sound made by the enemy creeping in.

Peeking at an angle from the loophole he manned, the Rio Kid caught the sudden ruby flare of a torch as it was lit and hurled at the roof of the cabin. He shot his carbine at the spot where he had first seen it, and heard the grunt of a man taking the bullet.

"Roof's sod," Wyatt Earp whispered, across the cabin. "Won't catch fire easy."

But a dozen lighted brands were simultaneously thrown at the log walls. They burned on the ground, licking against the bark of the logs. Smoke began to obscure the clearing.

"What say we sally out and fight our way through while we got the chance, Wyatt?" Red suggested gruffly.

"Better stick where we are," Earp said tonelessly.

He knew that young Celestino could not stand such a dash. Like Bob Pryor, he was willing to stay and die rather than desert the Mexican boy.

Increasing activity kept them busy at the loopholes. Braves were running up, and one managed to throw a burning torch into the interior of the cabin. Earp shot down the savage while Pryor stamped out the fire.

"They're comin'!" Pryor announced. "Get ready, boys!"

Dark forms sprang up all around the shack, charging at the building. The guns roared fast in the hut as Celestino loaded swiftly. But they could not keep this up forever. Weariness was gripping the fighting men, and their ammunition was being burnt up at a rapid rate.

Wyatt Earp, wiping sweat off his bronzed forehead, suddenly gave a quick exclamation.

"Yuh hear that, Red?" he demanded.

From the west came the sound of heavy guns. Experts like the Rio Kid and Earp could instantly identify the difference in these reports and those made by the Indians' rifles.

"Buffalo guns!" Pryor exclaimed, and Red swore excitedly.

Eagerly they listened while heavy volleys smashed one after the other. The direct attack from the Indians and Tank Loman's killers slowed, broke.

From the western loophole, the beleaguered men could see the red-yellow flashes of the heavier rifles.

"Those are Sharps!" declared Bob Pryor.

A wild yell, from fighting men's throats, burst over the sounds of the battle.

"White men — buffalo hunters!" Red shouted, jumping up and down in the joy of relief.

Volley after volley smashed into gleaming, painted bodies of the attacking Indians. Pryor, Earp and Red shot with a new fervor to help break the foe.

137

Startlingly close at hand a deep voice bawled over the din:

"Hey, who's inside there? That you, Wyatt Earp?"

"Yeah, Cody — four of us here," replied Earp, and quickly explained to the Rio Kid: "That's Bill Cody — feller they call Buffalo Bill, 'count he supplies buffalo beef to the railroad men. Friend of mine. Asked me to join his party, but I'd rather hunt alone."

"Damn yuh for that!" Red said with sardonic humor. "My scalp's half loose right now, Earp."

Spread out, but keeping in a rough skirmish line, came thirty white men, led by a tall, handsome man in buckskin clothes and moccasins. One of the buckskin men dropped, another leaped from his horse and stood firing.

The terrific volleys from their heavy Sharps rifles tore into the redskins. They turned, broke and fled for the cover of the forest, with the yelling hunters following them up and giving them a good start.

Wyatt Earp threw up the heavy bar and pulled back the thick door to welcome his friends, the buffalo hunters. Scouts were out, watching the edges of the clearing, but the Indians did not return. Burning brands threw a reddish glow over the space near the little cabin whose thick walls had served the quartet so well.

"Buffalo Bill" Cody, stalwart, and with brown hair long under his curved felt Stetson, and wearing fringed buckskin, grinned as he faced Wyatt Earp.

"So yuh wouldn't join up with us, Wyatt?" he jibed. " 'No, thanks, I'd ruther hunt alone'!"

The famous scout's brown eyes twinkled merrily as he thrust out a hand to Earp.

"Well," drawled Earp, "I did wanna hunt alone, Cody, but the Indians wouldn't let me. They come without an invitation."

More hunters strolled up to greet the men they had snatched from red death. One was a slim, eager youth with a round head and quick blue eyes. Buffalo Bill seized his shoulder and pushed him forward.

"Here's young Bat Masterson, Wyatt," he said. "Couldn't make him stay behind."

Bat Masterson, yet to make his great name as a Western marshal on the frontier but already an A-1 shot and hunter accepted the attention a little sheepishly. He carried a buffalo gun as long as himself, which he handled gingerly, for it was still hot from shooting.

"Howdy suh," he said to Earp and nodded to the lank lone hunter and to the Rio Kid.

He was only about Celestino Mireles' age, a boy whom the hard, savage life of the wilderness had made a man overnight, but he had pioneer blood in him and the innate power, not yet developed, of the great fighting man he was to become.

Buffalo Bill's brown goatee and mustache sheening in the light of the blaze they lit to cook up some meat, squatted on the ground in the circle of whites, listening to the tale Red told of the fight.

"And so yuh horned in and saved this gent," he said, nodding at Bob Pryor, the Rio Kid.

"Well, what would you do," asked Red, "if a feller run up to yuh with a pack of wolves after him?"

The hunters had food and drink. Their horses were close at hand, but they explained that their wagons were some miles west where they had been shooting during the day.

"Heard yore gunfire this afternoon while we were out makin' a stand," explained Cody. "We come over right away and got here before dark, but we waited till the Indians came out in the open 'fore we hit 'em." He lifted his mug. "Here's how, boys!

140

Let's drink while we can."

Bob Pryor fitted in with these strong frontiersmen. They were his own kind. He listened to the talk of the buffalo, of the Indians they had to fight in the Territory and on the Kansas plains.

"Custer and Sheridan are right put out," Cody reported. "There have been more and more raids on the towns ahead of the track layers, west of Abilene." He was thoughtfully quiet a moment. "Umm, wonder where those devils tonight got their new guns?" he said ruminatively.

"I savvy that," the Rio Kid drawled. "White men furnished 'em, so they could hit our herd."

Quickly he told of the vicious massacre on the Chisholm Trail. Buffalo Bill shook his handsome head when the Kid finished, his voice vibrant with angry emotion.

"Yuh'll never see them cows again, Kid," Cody said flatly. "They'll switch the brands if they want to sell 'em. Mebbe the Indians will eat 'em themselves."

"Yuh any idea where that tribe's from?" asked Pryor.

"Shore, shore," Cody answered. "Yuh can tell by their tribal markin's. They belong to a village and tribe run by a half-breed devil named Virgil Colorado. That is, most of 'em

141

do. Here, look at this body, though. That man's no Indian!"

The corpses of the enemy fighters lay about the clearing, for the Indians had not had time to carry off all their dead, so sudden and overwhelming had been the attack of the rescue party under the shrewd Buffalo Bill. Bob Pryor strolled over to the body which Cody indicated. Buffalo Bill squatted by the dead man, studying the corpse. Eagle feathers decorated the head, and the face was painted and darkly stained, but Cody quickly rubbed some of the berry juice from the evil countenance.

Bob Pryor stared at the features in the light of the brand which young Bat Masterson had brought from the fire.

"It's one of Tank Loman's gunmen," he told Earp and Cody.

"There's no use tryin' to trace those cows, Kid," Cody repeated sympathetically. "Yore Texas friends'll have to take their loss. Virgil Colorado's men are a good many miles off their usual huntin' grounds and it's a fair bet they're up to more than the usual devilment. I noticed most of 'em are young braves — reckless devils who can be primed to any kind of dirty work. Lucretia Borgia here" — he patted his needle gun, his favorite weapon — "has taken care of plenty such, gentlemen. Now, Earp, you and the Rio Kid here better join up with our party. It's fair and square. Every man takes a share of the total we make on the hunt. It's safer to stick together in this country."

Bob Pryor thanked the famous scout, but refused.

"I reckon I'll be ridin' in the mornin', after I'd had a rest," he drawled. "I got work to do on the trail."

His heart bled for the ruined Texans of Rose Valley, for the women and men who had lost their young sons. Something *must* be done for them!

Chapter XII:
Back from the Dead

In a daze of agony Herb Malcom woke to a red nightmare of pain, pain that tore at his vitals. He tried to speak, to move, but he could not.

The sun was high, warming him as its rays penetrated to the deep thickets in which he lay.

"Boys — watch yoreselves!" he tried to call, but had no voice, beyond a faint whisper.

He had come back to his senses at the mental point where he had left off when, trying to reach the great cattle herd, and calling his men after him, he had ridden through the circle of attacking Indians into the darkness.

A fusillade had rattled through the leaves of the bushes and trees, as he rode. Two had struck, the first only biting a chunk of flesh from his scalp, but the second had driven into his body close to the shoulder, piercing deep.

He was paralyzed now, could not shift himself from the uncomfortable position in which he lay. His chestnut mustang, stung by a bullet sent in the same volley which had got Malcom, had made a wild dash through the darkness. His rider, unconscious from that blinding blow the lead slug had dealt his head, clung to the leather by sheer instinct for a half mile. Then the overhanging branch of a tree had swept Malcom off the chestnut, to come crashing down into a dense thicket of thorny bushes.

The horse galloped on, as Herb Malcom lay there unconscious, unaware of the awful battle in which all of his friends, save for the Rio Kid and Celestino Mireles, were slaughtered, raged on in the night.

Trailing Indians, following cows and those horses which had broken loose, failed to ferret out the trail boss, hidden in the center of the bush. Tossed from the mustang into the middle of this chaparral, there had been no tracks left and no signs to show that anyone had entered, as would have been the case had a wounded man crawled through.

Malcom's head was splitting; he was perishing for a drink of water. Visions floated before his blurred sight. He was growing delirious, believed he was talking to Betsy White, the girl he loved.

"Here I am, back again, Betsy," he whispered. "Sold the cows at a good price, got plenty to pay all we owe to Barrett for stakin' us. Reckon we're on the way to riches."

Though he could not guess it, it was fortunate he could not move, and could only whisper. For the Chisholm Trail was close, and along it came the Rose Valley herd, driven by rough-looking white men, and a number of Indians.

Malcom heard the sounds the herd made, the bellowings of the cattle, the thudding of hoofs on the earth. With blurred eyes, he peered through the interstices of bush, out into the sunlight of the Trail. He saw the familiar cattle plodding by, animals individualized for him in the long drive from Texas. Among the flankers he noted a broad, squat white man with one arm bandaged — a man with a bulbous nose and dirty straw-colored mustache.

"Dog Donnolly!" he muttered, and struggled desperately to rise.

The effort exhausted him. He lost his senses again. When he awoke, night had laid her mantle over the wilderness, quiet save for the mournful wail of a coyote.

Stiffness was his main trouble, now, for

146

his head felt clearer. The body wound had done the real damage to the trail boss' powerful system. His head was better, though clotted blood tangled his hair. Still he could move his body a little, and make motions with hands and feet. Not enough to help himself though, and Herb Malcom realized with a pang that, lying in a pool of his own blood, he could only wait for the end.

Later he slept, feverishly. The sun was up high when he waked again.

A sound filtered to him and he fought for clearness of head and vision. Suddenly into his restricted range of vision came a horseman, a tall man in buckskins and Stetson, riding a black mustang. A rifle was across his saddle horn, and he was on the alert.

Malcom did not recognize him. Then came a second man, and at sight of him Herb Malcom's heart leaped. It was the Rio Kid, on Saber, the mouse-colored dun with the black stripe along his backbone!

"Kid, Kid!" Malcom tried to call, but he was unable to raise his voice high enough to make himself heard.

With horrible agony, Malcom saw the Rio Kid passing on. Desperation gave him the strength to do what he did then. He got hold of a dry bush limb near one hand and put all he had left into shaking it, moving his feet at the same time.

The Rio Kid, hearing the rustle of the brush to his left as he scouted along the Chisholm Trail for sign of the red raiders, swung in his saddle, his gun flashing into his quick hand.

Ready for trouble on the instant, he stared at the spot from which the suspicious sounds had come.

"What's wrong, Kid?" demanded Wyatt Earp, swinging quickly, his own gun up.

"Somethin' in that bush clump," growled Pryor, never taking his eyes off the spot.

He had left Celestino Mireles with Buffalo Bill Cody's party. The Mexican youth needed rest and care for a few days, until he could gather his strength, and give his wound a chance to heal.

Wyatt Earp, heading back to see what had happened to his wagonloads of buffalo hides, had found them untouched. The Indian raiders eager on the trail of more victims had been in too much of a hurry to take Earp's wagons along, intending to pick them up on their way back. But the arrival of the many buffalo hunters had driven the redskins off.

Earp had offered to scout the Chisholm Trail with the Kid. They had looked over the scene of that terrible massacre. Scalped bodies, awful in their nakedness, lay about. Everything of value had been taken; horses, gear, the great cattle herd. Earp and the Kid had stopped long enough to give the victims decent burial, until they could later be removed to their Texas homes, and had been taking the trail again when the Kid had heard the sound in the brush that had brought him up short.

Edging Saber closer to the spot from which the noises had come, the Rio Kid once again heard the unmistakable, though faint, rustle of the dry bush leaves.

He dismounted and quickly went toward the gnarled live-oak one long extending branch of which had swept Herb Malcom's body from his mustang in the night. Cautiously parting the thorn bushes with his left hand, his Colt revolver up and gripped ready in his right, the Kid glimpsed the black, muddy halfboots of a man. He recognized the roweled Spanish spurs instantly. They were Herb Malcom's!

He cursed as he leaped in, oblivious of the tearing barbs of the chaparral. An instant later he was bending over the young trail boss, and Wyatt Earp, hustling over on his horse, answered the Rio Kid's call.

"Bring a canteen, Earp!" Pryor ordered.

"Here's one of 'em — Herb Malcom!"

"Ain't he dead?" asked Earp, kicking the entrance path larger with his leather-covered legs, and passing the canteen in to the Kid.

"Nope, but nigh onto it."

Frontiersmen that they were, both the Kid and Wyatt Earp could size up a bullet wound, tell how dangerous it was. His training in the Civil War had taught Pryor a great deal. His face was grave as he estimated Malcom's injuries.

"The one on his head's nothin' but a crease," he reported. "But the one under his shoulder-blade is bad. Bullet's still in and interferin' with his left lung. C'mon, help me tote him."

They carried the weak Malcom into the sunlight, laid him gently on the grass. Thorns had cut his flesh, and he was terribly bruised. The Kid poured water between the swollen, pallid lips. It was minutes before their first-aid helped the trail boss to stir, then open pain-racked eyes.

"Rio Kid — Rio Kid!" he whispered huskily. "Are — they all dead?"

"All but me and Celestino." The Kid's mouth was a grim line and there was tragedy in his deep-blue eyes. "But you'll get well, Herb. Jest take it easy."

"But the cows — our herd —"

"Never mind them. It wasn't yore fault."

"Yes, yes! I — I was in charge. . . . I saw Dog Donnolly drivin' 'em north — Loman and him are in on it — up the Trail. . . . We'll lose Rose Valley now —"

He shuddered, and collapsed once more. Pryor swung to Earp. "He needs a good sawbones quick as we can get him to one, Wyatt. What's the best place?"

"Well, this young feller'll die if yuh jolt him long on a hoss, Kid," the tall, somber Earp replied. "Tell yuh what. I got a good load of hides on my wagon, and we'll make Malcom a bed on 'em and I'll leave him with the army surgeon at Fort Gibson on the Arkansas River."

"Good!" Pryor agreed. "That's on the way to Abilene. I'm headin' for there, Earp, for I reckon Tank Loman and Donnolly'll rush them stole beeves to market fast as they can run 'em."

Earp nodded. "They got a long start, Kid," he said soberly. "If they push the cows and don't mind runnin' some fat off 'em, yuh'll never catch up with 'em."

"Mebbe not," drawled Bob Pryor. "But I kin try."

"Yuh'll have to stick here with Malcom till I fetch back the wagons," Wyatt Earp told him. "It'll take some time, Kid. Red'll drive one. I can drive the other."

"All right, go to it. Soon as yuh load Malcom, I'll be headin' north on Loman's trail."

"Yuh're a brave man, Rio Kid," said Earp, and there was a slight commendatory smile touching his thin kips. "But it seems to me yuh're buckin' a tough game. This Loman's a slick rascal, and it's plain he's workin' with Virgil Colorado. So watch out how yuh tread on their heels. Savvy?"

Chapter XIII:
City of the Plains

Doggedly Bob Pryor, the Rio Kid, pushed his mud-caked horse Saber, the dun with the black stripe along his backbone, across Mud Creek, heading into Abilene, City of the Plains.

Behind the Kid lay miles of trail. Twice he had been fired on from ambush, and he had a new wound where a bullet from a skulking foe had clipped a chunk from his shoulder. The speed of his trip had been broken by enemies evidently watching for him, set by Tank Loman and others who did not wish the Kid to overtake the Rose Valley trail herd that was being driven swiftly north to market. Forced to detour, pursued through the wilderness by wild-riding Indians, the Rio Kid had been unable to catch up with Dog Donnolly and Tank Loman, who were with the cattle.

Dusk was near as the Kid headed into the wild-and-woolly cowtown, biggest of cattle markets. For tens of miles south of Abilene cattle herds were quartered, guarded by cowboys and ready for buyers. The railroad pens were filled with steers which had been driven from all parts of the West to this great market. Thousands on thousands of hoof-marks cut up the plains for miles about the town.

Abilene had been laid out in 1860, a handful of shacks. The City of the Plains had grown but slowly its first half decade, when it was known as Station Number Two on the Butterfield Overland Despatch between Denver and Atchison. In 1867, Abilene was a small, dead place composed of a dozen log huts with sod roofs. But in that year the Kansas Pacific Railroad was building west from Kansas City, and reached Abilene in the spring.

One Joseph McCoy established a shipping station for Texas longhorns, and the town became the favorite shipping point for the drovers. Astounding changes took place in the small sleepy settlement, almost over-night. Hotels, stores, boarding houses, a dozen saloons and business places opened up to take care of the cattle trade.

Immediately Abilene was the liveliest town in the West, filled with drovers, cattle buyers, commission men and speculators in beef. A motley army of toughs flocked in to prey on the cowmen, and Abilene had more killers to the square yard than any town on the continent.

The Rio Kid looked on the bustling scene as he decided on his next move in tracing the Rose Valley herd. Most of the buildings were of one story, he observed, though some had two or even three floors. But as each builder had gone about construction in his own way and usually in a hurry, the town as a whole presented a crooked, uneven aspect.

South of the K.P. tracks was Texas Abilene, and the Rio Kid nodded as he recognized the names of the big saloons and gambling places — Planters Hotel, the Bull's Head, with a big sign reading:

WELCOME TEXAS!
PROPS. BEN THOMPSON AND
PHIL COE!

Around the corner on Cedar Street was the Alamo, headquarters of Marshal "Wild Bill" Hickok. On A Street, facing the railroad tracks, were four saloons in a row and the well known Drovers' Cottage Hotel. And along the railroad were located the stockyards covering acres of land, and filled with bellowing cattle. Adjoining the yards on the east edge of the town was "Devil's Half-acre," the toughest section.

The men, wearing cowmen's clothing and muddy halfboots, mingled with black-frocked, somber gamblers and painted, smiling saloon girls. Here were sporting men, desperadoes, and bullwhackers, toughest of the tough; now and then soldiers on leave, or a frontier scout in from the plains and mountains.

"Bear River" Tom Smith, Abilene's first famous marshal, had been shot and killed not long before when he had sought to arrest two killers in a dugout on Chapman Creek, a few miles northeast of Abilene, and Wild Bill Hickok had been called to take his place.

Night dropped over the prairie land. Hundreds on hundreds of oil lamps were lighted, candles supplementing them. Bob Pryor, the Rio Kid, was hungry and tired from the terrific strain under which he had ridden for so long. Saber, too, needed attention. The Kid prized his mount above himself and, dismounting, he led the spirited dun into the largest and best looking livery stable at hand. A grooming and grain feed were in order for Saber, after watering.

Pryor checked his six-guns and stretched his stiffened limbs, crossing the street and ducking under the hitch-rail among the crowds of citizens coming out for the evening. A barber shop was his first stop and a shave, a haircut, and bath made him again the spruce, arrow-straight Rio Kid. Next stop was a restaurant, where he consumed a double order of ham and eggs, coffee and dessert.

"Reckon Tank Loman'll try to sell them beeves here," he decided, as he left the eating place. "Have to locate him first of all."

With this idea in mind, he walked the streets, looking in saloons and public spots for the tall Loman. It was around ten P.M. when, crossing the dirt road, dodging horsemen who galloped recklessly up and down, he glimpsed a familiar figure.

"It ain't Loman, but he'll do," the Kid muttered, for he had spotted the squat mule skinner, Dog Donnolly.

A blare of bright lights, sounds of raucous voices and clinking glasses came from the wide-open doors of the big Bull's Head Saloon nearby. Dog Donnolly was just entering the place, and the Rio Kid followed a few steps behind.

Music came from the dancehall at one side. In the back were the gaming rooms, where the players sat silently at their tables. The Kid, pausing in the door, saw Dog

Donnolly weaving through to the rear over the sawdust-covered floor. Trailing after him, the Kid came close to a tall man, with a swarthy complexion and blue eyes who was clad in the finest clothing money could buy. He had a sweeping mustache, curly hair, and stood very straight. He was laughing as he told a story.

"That's a good 'un, Ben," roared a listening sycophant.

But Thompson, the famous gambler, half-owner of the Bull's Head, nodded, and swung toward the back rooms.

Goin' to work, boys," he announced pleasantly. The sharp eyes shot a quick glance at the Rio Kid who was quietly heading after Dog Donnolly. "Guns checked with the barkeeper, Mister," he called.

The Rio Kid knew something of Ben Thompson who, because he had killed a man when he was thirteen, boasted the doubtful distinction of being the youngest "man" ever indicted for murder in Texas.

Gambler and gunfighter, Thompson had proved a constant trouble-maker in the Confederate Army during the war. He had been in many shooting scrapes, and finally had been sent to prison for killing a man. Released, he had come to Abilene and run a few dollars up to a large stake, in a faro

game. This money he had invested in the
Bull's Head. With his partner, Phil Coe, he
had bought the best equipment to be obtained. A gold mine could not have been
more profitable than the Bull's Head.

"Sorry," the Rio Kid replied evenly, as
Thompson addressed him, "but I'm goin'
to need my guns."

At the sound of his voice, Dog Donnolly
whirled. The broad, flat face of the squat
mule skinner flushed beet-red as he saw the
Rio Kid. Instantly he whipped out his revolver.

The Rio Kid made a draw of his ready
Colt that was lightning. Ben Thompson had
not seen Donnolly's draw. He believed that
Pryor was drawing on him, and the speed
of the Rio Kid with his gun sent the gambler's hands quickly up, his blue eyes nar-
rowing. Then as quickly he realized that the
Kid was not gunning him, but someone
behind him.

Donnolly's gun flamed, but Bob Pryor's
Colt had spoken a shade ahead of the mule
skinner's.

"Why, damn yuh!" yelped Ben Thompson.

He had felt the wind of the bullets, the
Rio Kid's, speeding past at waist level to
drive into Dog Donnolly's belly, the squat

killer's slugs biting a chunk from Thompson's boot heel as it buried itself in the saloon floor.

With a choking curse, Donnolly dropped his gun, hands flying to his stomach. He doubled up and crashed in a heap in the passageway to the rear.

Immediately the Bull's Head became a madhouse, as everybody tried to get out of bullet range. Men ducked behind the bar, under tables. Those near enough spurted out the door. Yells and screams of women rose up.

"Yuh fool, yuh killed him!" snarled Ben Thompson, angry because the riot was bad for business.

"Keep yore hands in sight, Thompson," ordered Pryor quietly. " 'Twas self-defense."

Thompson said nothing more. Two seconds later, as the Rio Kid quickly stepped past the gambler, heading for the back, Tank Loman and a dozen men burst from a rear door into the hall.

"There he is — the Rio Kid!" bawled Loman.

Loman's hand flashed for his gun, his men followed suit, bunched thick about him. The Rio Kid leaped back from the narrow passage, foreseeing the deadly volley that came an instant later. As the Kid made the turn, he shot once, hoping to get Loman, but the big fellow was covered by one of his eager gunnies, who took the slug in his thigh. The crack of the bone as the bullet broke it sounded sharp above the rising din.

Ben Thompson, expert at such affrays, had leaped behind the end of the bar and was reaching for a gun kept hidden under the counter.

The Kid snapped a bullet at the angry gambler, cutting splinters from the bar top to force Thompson to stop his attempt to get his gun.

"Hold it, gents!" shouted Pryor. "I'm on my way!"

Tank Loman was urging his gunnies into the saloon to finish off the Rio Kid. Pryor dusted the doorway of the passage with bullets that tore off chunks of painted wood and clouded plaster fragments into the eyes of the snarling fighting men from Texas. He jumped back through an open window, and struck soft earth under the sill.

"Stop him!" shrieked Tank Loman. "Get him! Shot a man in cold blood!"

More cries rang out, as the hot blood of excited men surged high:

"Get him. . . . Lynch the dirty killer. . . . Go round to the front. . . . Look out, he'll shoot through the winder!"

161

The Rio Kid sprang up from the ground and turned toward Tin Can Alley, behind the Bull's Head. Men stuck heads and shoulders through windows, firing after him in the darkness. Pryor hustled around back of the building next the saloon, cut up through a space between two houses, intending to cross and reach the stable where Saber was resting.

But as he came out onto the awninged sidewalk, a man standing close against the wall, on a low porch, shoved an ivory-handled pistol into his back.

"Yuh damn Texas man!" the man growled. "Drop —"

The Rio Kid's eyes took in his captor who, mistaking his movement that meant surrender, struck him a hard blow with the heavy revolver barrel. The Kid fell forward on his face in the dirt, a million lights flashing before his stunned vision.

Chapter XIV:
Marshal of Abilene

Lying on a wooden bench behind the steel bars of a jail cell, Bob Pryor's head cleared slowly. The first thing he discovered was that his guns, the two in the cartridge belt and the two under his armpits, had been removed. A confused sound which at first the Rio Kid took to be the roaring of his own blood in his ears, resolved into what he finally identified as the noise a large mob of angry men makes — he had heard such hell-born choruses before, in the army, during his scouting trips as one of Custer's aides in the Civil War.

"Sounds like that time at Frederick," he muttered, wiping dirt and sweat from his face with a sweep of his hand.

At Frederick, on one of his dangerous expeditions for General Custer's cavalry, Pryor had come upon a mob of Southerners who had caught a suspected spy, and had helplessly watched while the fellow was lynched. He recognized the same deep threatening notes in the sounds made by the crowd storming outside the new Abilene lockup.

"Reckon it's me that they want this time," he muttered.

He struggled to his feet and went to the barred door of his cell. Just before he reached it a tall figure slouched by the barred door. He recognized the man to whom he had tried to surrender, the man who had jumped him when he had come out of the alley after his escape from the Bull's Head, Ben Thompson's emporium of pleasure.

His captor, seeing he was awake, strolled toward him, scowling with hard eyes. They were eyes of power and absolutely fearless.

The man was tall and erect, and long brown hair swept in profusion to the tops of his shoulders. He had a long, curved nose, rather narrow, high cheek bones and a noble brow. At the moment he was attired in "city duds," a Mississippi River steamboat gambler's getup of long-tailed black cutaway coat, wide blue pants tapering at the bottom where showed high-heeled boots with the spurs removed. A wide leather belt supported two ivory-handled cap-and-ball Colt revolvers. His white shirt was spotless, and the black string tie was carefully arranged. The strong face was adorned with a flowing, drooping mustache, and altogether the man had the poise and confidence of one who can take care of himself and knows it.

"Well, Texas man," he growled, "so yuh got caught at yore deviltry. Hear 'em outside? They're howlin' for yore blood."

"Yuh're Marshal Wild Bill Hickok, ain't yuh?" Pryor asked quietly. "I saw yore marshal's star and meant to surrender, but —"

The tall erect man only answered the question.

"That's what they call me."

At that time, James Butler Hickok, familiarly called "Wild Bill," was in the prime of his fighting power. He ruled Abilene with an iron hand and the man who dared go against him was either a fool or drunk, for his speed with guns, his high courage and readiness to fight it out when challenged, were famous.

The noise of the mob was growing louder. Stones were banging ominously on the thick oak panels of the doors.

"Them fellers'll tear yuh to pieces if they get hold of yuh," Wild Bill remarked, closely observing the cool man in the cell.

Bob Pryor shrugged. In all his fighting

165

days, nothing like fear had ever overcome him yet.

"I'd feel better if I had my guns," he drawled. "Got the makin's? I'd like a smoke."

Wild Bill Hickok silently handed him a sack of tobacco and brown cigarette papers, and the Rio Kid rolled a smoke.

The marshal strode to the window and looked out.

"Ben Thompson's out there, hottin' 'em up," he informed. "His crazy brother Bill's jest come up, too — got a skinful, and that generally means hell to pay."

Contempt was in Hickok's voice as he spoke of the Thompsons. He had a feud of his own with Ben Thompson and his partner, Phil Coe.

"Thompson's no friend of mine," the Kid told the marshal frankly. "I went in the Bull's Head after a cattle rustler and killer named Dog Donnolly. Donnolly saw me, jerked his gun, and I beat him to it. That's the truth, Marshal. And 'fore yuh let that mob out there do their tearin' of me, I want to tell yuh that Donnolly worked for a feller named Tank Loman — mebbe yuh know him — and Loman egged Virgil Colorado's renegade Indians on to attack a cattle herd me and my friends from Rose Valley, Texas,

166

were drivin' up the Trail."

"Yuh're a Texas man yoreself, though." The marshal shook his head. "They always make trouble here."

"Yeah, I come from Texas. They call me the Rio Kid."

"Soldier, too. I see that. Fought against us in the war."

"I rode for Custer," said the Kid simply.

Hickok, a man with decided prejudices, and one who knew his own mind, grunted as he stared hard at Pryor.

"Custer's a good man," he admitted, "though some of his soldiers need takin' down. The general's not far from town jest now — in camp southwest of here. Been tryin' to meet up with a bunch of renegade Creeks." He paused thoughtfully, then went on: "I didn't savvy why Ben Thompson was after yuh, seein' as how yuh're a Texas man too. Reckon yuh're no pard of his, but mebbe the man yuh dropped was. Mebbe Ben's jest mad 'cause yuh shot up his honkytonk, but anyhow it's excitin' sport, lynchin' a man. . . . Jest how did yuh say that killin' of Donnolly happened? They claim you shot first."

"I did," the Rio Kid said promptly, "but Donnolly drew ahead of me, Marshal. Not many saw him go for his gun, 'cause he was in the passage and it was dim."

"Fair and square, then." Wild Bill was musing, watching the Rio Kid, trying to figure it out right. "Yeah, I know Loman and I knew Donnolly, too — a couple of bad hombres, if they ever was any. Now listen! This mob won't get yuh, except over my dead body. However, if yuh stay here for trial, Loman and his pards, and Ben Thompson, too, will shore swear yuh kilt Dog in cold blood."

A heavy banging sounded on the door.

"Hey, Marshal Hickok!" a gruff voice roared. "I seen that skunk shoot Donnolly! If yuh want a witness, I'm one, and here's a dozen more seen the whole thing."

Wild Bill winked at Pryor.

"Who's that?" he called.

"Tank Loman," the man outside called back. "Let's try him right now, Marshal! He's guilty as hell."

Hickok hitched up his gun-belt, the white-handled Colts gleaming in the lamplight as he crossed to the door. He unbolted it and stood, arms akimbo, facing the raging mob. At sight of the marshal, they quieted somewhat and those in front were not so eager to press forward. They began stepping back on the toes of the crushers behind them.

"Go on — take that killer!" voices in the

rear yelled, but nobody seemed to wish to be the first to try it.

Tank Loman stood on the stone stoop, scowling, his fierce eyes gleaming reddish in the flickering light. Behind him were a number of his followers, heavily armed.

"So, Loman, yuh admit I'm Marshal of Abilene, do yuh?" Wild Bill drawled.

"Shore," growled Tank, bristling. "And if yuh're worth yore salt, yuh'll let us see justice done."

"I agree with yuh," said Wild Bill, and calmly slapped Loman in the mouth with all the force of his strong arm.

The crack of Hickok's hand against the sullen gunman's lips sounded as sharp as a pistol shot. The lip was driven against the yellowed teeth, and blood spurted from the cut flesh.

"Now go lie down, yuh dirty dog," Hickok said.

His slim hands hung loose at his sides. Had Tank Loman made a move for his gun, he would have died then and there. But Loman knew, too well, the legendary speed of Wild Bill Hickok's draw. A deep flush spread beneath the tan of his cheeks, and he choked out a curse. But across his eyes flashed a filming yellow light. He could not stand up to Hickok's terrible gaze.

"Loman's yeller," flashed across the Rio Kid's mind with no surprise. The impression he had gathered when he had first run across the big gunny was now confirmed. "He's a killer all right, but he don't take no chances when he ain't got the upper hand. He's no shore enough fightin' man — he's just a bluff. No feller would take what he jest did from the marshal a-layin' down, less'n he was pure polecat."

Abrupt silence fell over the crowd after the marshal's blow. Cursing under his breath, Tank Loman swung on his heels and strode through the crowd, followed by his muttering band of gunmen. Wild Bill's lips were curved in a sneer.

"Anybody else want an argument?" he bawled.

Ben Thompson sprang up on a wagon stone.

"Yeah, I do!" he yelled.

Another man, younger, taller, and slimmer, his face working with excitement, jumped up beside the saloon man.

"Me, too, Hickok!" he yelped. "Yuh danged fourflushin' polecat!"

"Them words is compliments from you, Bill," Hickok called contemptuously.

"Shush, Bill," Ben ordered. There was nothing yellow about Ben Thompson. He hated Hickok, and did not fear to fling his defiance in the marshal's face. "Yuh take too much on yoreself in this town, Hickok!" he yelled. "One of these days yuh'll pay for it, savvy?"

"That a threat?" sneered Wild Bill.

"Yes, it's a threat! And yuh can like it or lump it! I'm a friend of the Texas men and yuh're playin' favorites against us."

"Send yore bill now," cried Hickok, and took a step forward.

Ben Thompson was furious, but he showed no yellow streak, facing the great gunfighter.

"We'll get that killer legal, tomorrer!" he roared.

"Second the motion," shrieked his brother Bill and, drawing a .45 Colt, he pulled the trigger.

His bullet whipped through the leaves of the live-oak near at hand. Bill Thompson was in high spirits, delighting in such a scene.

"I'll git a marshal tonight!" he bellowed. "I swore I would!"

His gun was dropping. Even if he missed Hickok, if he fired again, he would surely wound someone in the crowd. Wild Bill's ivory-handled Colt flashed into action with the speed of legerdemain. It spat once, and

Bill Thompson's gun flew out of his hand and hit the dirt. Bill screamed with rage and pain, as he grabbed his bruised fingers.

"Damn yuh — damn yuh!" he raved. "I'll —"

"Get him home to bed, Thompson!" shouted Hickok to the saloon man. "If I hear him again tonight I'll lock him up."

He swung, slammed the door in the mob's face, and with a grin turned back to the Rio Kid.

"That's the way to treat such scum," he said.

An hour passed, during which the crowd, tired of waiting and none daring to take the initiative in storming the jail under Wild Bill's guns, began melting back to wet throats dry from yelling. Hickok sat down in a wooden chair, feet up against the wall. He and the Rio Kid smoked and talked an hour longer.

"How 'bout that stolen herd?" Bob Pryor asked, after a time. "Can anything be done about it?"

Wild Bill shrugged. "The Chisholm Trail's none of my jurisdiction, Kid. Anyhow yuh only got a hunch that Loman was ridin' with Colorado's Injuns. Yuh can't prove yuh seen him. Yuh're wanted here for murder, and there's nothin' I can do. If them cows

172

ain't shipped East yet, with their brands switched, they will be 'fore yuh can get any action."

He arose again and looked out.

"Coast is clear now," he said, after a long survey. "Now, if yuh stick in town, Kid, as I was a-sayin', Ben Thompson'll see yuh hung jest to spite me. This Loman makes his headquarters at the Bull's Head and pays plenty for it, so even though Ben ain't in on the thievery, he'll be for Loman as a customer and a Texas man. Yuh got no chance in this town. I believe yore story, Kid, and I'm goin' to let yuh go free."

"Won't that make trouble for yuh?" the Kid asked quickly, and the marshal grinned wryly.

"As Thompson was jest a-sayin'," Wild Bill drawled, "they can like it or lump it. I'll explain to the mayor and the committee. They hire me. I'm backin' yuh against Thompson and his crowd, savvy? But don't let me see yuh again in Abilene. If I do I'll have to arrest yuh. Now I'm goin'. See them keys on that hook? A man with a good stretch could jest about reach 'em from the cell yuh're in."

Wild Bill deliberately hung the keys on the nearby hook to suit his words.

"Where's yore hoss, Kid?" he asked.

173

Pryor told him and Hickok went on: "That back door can be unbolted. In one hour there might be a hoss waitin' outside. Yuh might get away."

He nodded, and left by the front way.

CHAPTER XV:
TRAIL RENDEZVOUS

Midnight had come, and had long since gone when the Rio Kid, stretching to his fullest extent, got his hand on the cell keys, and in a moment had let himself out of the cell. Across the large room his cartridge belt, with his guns in the holsters, hung from a wooden peg. He strapped it on, and unbolted the back portal. Cautiously he stepped out into the dark alley.

A shadowy horse stood close at hand.

"Saber!" the Kid said softly, and the dun answered with a sniff, nuzzling his hand.

With the powerful, lightning-fast dun under him, the Rio Kid was himself again. He rode along Tin Can Alley and cut south across the tracks toward Mud Creek. Behind him stood Abilene, its Biblical name sadly besmudged by the men and women who inhabited it. The town still blazed with lamplight, and the saloons and honkytonks were bedlams of raucous sound.

Back there, somewhere in the vast pens, the Rio Kid guessed the Rose Valley herd must be held, and he meant to do something about that, for the sake of the people of Rose Valley.

"Got to save them folks," he muttered.

But Abilene was gunning for him, and the going would be hard. Wild Bill would be compelled to arrest him if he entered the town again. And Tank Loman and all of Thompson's cronies would gladly shoot him on sight.

He swung along the creek bank, staring into the darkness in the direction of the cattle yards. Stock cars stood on the sidings, and in the darkness came the bellowings of many steers.

"Wonder if I could locate the herd?" he murmured.

It was like finding a needle in a haystack in the night. Cowboys guards were at the pens, watching over the animals. Lanterns burned here and there. Pryor, hunting along the line, suddenly heard a familiar voice. Just in time he drew Saber back into the shadows, against the bars of a filled pen, as though he were on night guard. He dropped his head, touching the dun so Saber would stand quiet.

"That's all settled, boys," Tank Loman

growled, not fifty feet from the Rio Kid. "C'mon, let's head south. Got to meet up with Colorado at dawn."

The gruff voices faded in the distance. A freight train, laden with cattle, was pulling out of Abilene, eastward for Chicago, the steers bellowing heavily at the unaccustomed movement

Bob Pryor swore, as he shoved Saber out and headed for the moving train.

"Figger our cows are sold and on their way to market," he muttered savagely.

He traveled as fast as he could through the yards, and his eagerness almost spelled his death. Close to the loading-pens sat half a dozen men on horseback. Lanterns gave light to the spot, and the glow fell across the Rio Kid's face as he pulled Saber to a sliding stop.

"Hey!" he shouted. "What brand's on them steers? I —"

"The Rio Kid!" shrieked one of the horsemen, diving for his gun.

More of Tank Loman's gunnies, the Kid instantly realized, probably set there to watch out for any interference.

He jerked hard on Saber's rein, and the great dun swerved and leaped over the bars into an empty pen. Guns flashed red-yellow in the night, seeking the Rio Kid. His single shot clipped one of Loman's crew, and the man's yells unnerved the rest, blinded by their own lights.

Saber jumped over the next fence, cut south between pens, and crossed the tracks.

The gunmen behind hunted the Rio Kid for a time, through the pens. But the doubling trick threw them off, and the Kid forded Mud Creek and headed away from town, hitting for the tall timber.

Tank Loman had beaten him, had sold the Rose Valley steers in record time, loaded them and pocketed the small fortune obtained from their sale.

"None of us was s'posed to ride out of that massacre," he growled furiously. "I reckon Loman's right uneasy 'bout me. Now I wonder where he's headin' next?"

He guessed that Loman had men with whom he worked, beside the gunnies who were his constant companions, perhaps superiors, because Tank Loman did not impress the Rio Kid as a man whose mentality was sufficient for him to be a leader. There was the connection with Virgil Colorado, of course, for which the Indian chief would demand payment, but there was no chance that Colorado was the guiding spirit of what appeared to be an organized gang of raiders.

The Rio Kid rode south on the main trail, not pressing too closely, for he guessed that Loman and his men were probably just ahead. At the first streaks of dawn the Rio Kid dismounted to investigate the fresh sign of half a dozen riders, and his suspicions were confirmed.

"Loman and his bunch all right," he mused.

Since it was so early, any cattle herds that might be approaching Abiline would be still bedded down off the Trail. It would probably be at such a time that Loman and his gunnies would strike.

Two miles south, Loman and his gunman band swung off the Trail and cut westward into the sagebrush. Following them, the Rio Kid proceeded cautiously, pausing occasionally to stare at the sky ahead with his narrowed, deep-blue eyes, trained to read every sign that would show the moves of his quarry.

Suddenly Saber sniffed, anxiously belligerently.

"Indian ponies, huh?" the Kid muttered. "Yeah, I reckon Tank's meetin' his pard Colorado this mornin', like he said, after sellin our cows."

A faint west wind brought with it the odor of frying beef. They were having breakfast, too.

Not daring to ride too close to the rendez-vous, the Kid left the dun and scouted through the brush afoot.

With ease he avoided the sentry left on the faint deer trail Loman had followed in, to the spot beside a little stream that meandered through the wilderness. The Kid crossed the brook above the spot where he could just catch the sound of those he sought, and came in from the south.

Bellying through the undergrowth for the last two hundred yards, in the growing light the Rio Kid peeked out to see Loman and Virgil Colorado, sitting together on the banks of the stream. Their men, redskins and Loman's gunnies, were consuming chunks of freshly cooked beef, cutting the meat with their hunting knives for each mouthful. Bottles of whiskey that had been brought by Loman's bunch were open, even for breakfast, and the Indians drank lustily.

"The boss told me to give yuh yore half," the Rio Kid heard Loman say to Colorado. "Sold the cows for forty thousand dollars."

Virgil Colorado shook his head. "Money no good to me," he growled. "You take, buy new guns, bullets, and whiskey, savvy? Deliver to me in six sleeps."

"All right," agreed Loman.

"Ugh! The Man Who Pretends and I have agreed. There are many more cattle on the Trail. With Indians' help you take them and sell them. That means more guns and bullets, and whiskey."

"Good!" Tank Loman cried enthusiastically. "We figgered yuh'd see it our way, Virgil. We'll raid the Chisholm Trail regular and nobody will be able to stop us once we get goin'."

"Only Pahuska," Colorado said laconically.

"Custer? Hell, the soldiers'll never catch up with yuh! I'll have my boys keep an eye on 'em and warn yuh when they ride. Then yuh can head for the mountains till they leave." He chuckled harshly. "Say," he remarked admiringly, "that's a plumb good name yuh got for the boss — the Man Who Pretends."

The Rio Kid ticketed what he overheard. So Loman and Virgil Colorado did have a hidden "boss" and with him, whoever he was, they were plotting wholesale destruction, murder and thievery on the Chisholm Trail. As plainly, too, the mysterious boss was pretending to be an Indian. And the success they had had with the Rose Valley herd had encouraged the devils.

Having overheard the enemy's plans, the

Rio Kid started his retreat. He inched away until he reached Saber, mounted, and rode back to the Chisholm Trail.

His practiced eye told him that someone was riding ahead of him. He pushed Saber on, carefully, until he came to a turn, where he could peer around and see who it was.

"Celestino!" he exclaimed, and shoved Saber forward.

The slim Mexican youth, riding a fast black horse, turned in his leather as he heard approaching hoofbeats, one hand dropping to the long knife in his sash.

"General!" he cried, reining in and whirling his horse.

"How are yuh, Celestino? Yuh strong enough to ride?"

"*Si, si,* General! I follow you to Abilene. I am well."

The Rio Kid looked the lad over. The boy was thin and peaked. His wound had taken a lot out of him.

"I'm headin' west, on a hard ride," he told Celestino.

"I go, too."

"No, you need rest — pronto. Yuh can help me by stayin' in Abilene, savvy? Tank Loman's in and out of there. Keep an eye on him, and yuh'll see him start out in a few days with a wagonload of contraband.

Trail 'em, and see where they go. Don't bump into Loman, though, whatever yuh do. He'll shoot yuh on sight. . . . Where's Wyatt Earp and Malcom?"

"Zey ha' gone to the Fort, to the east."

"Hope they make it. Now get goin', Celestino, and take care of yoreself. I'll connect with yuh along the Trail here within four days."

With a wave of his hand, the Rio Kid started young Mireles north. Then he pushed Saber westward along a buffalo track, heading into the wilds.

Chapter XVI:
Ruined Hopes

Fortified with the strength of determination, Herb Malcom, trail boss of the vanished Rose Valley herds, sat up on the edge of the army bunk at Fort Gibson, on the Arkansas.

Surrounded by a high palisade of sharpened stakes cut from hard woods, the fort consisted of a blockhouse looped for defense, barracks and officers' quarters, stores of ammunition and food cached for the use of the defenders, and a parade ground outside. The garrison was small, a handful of cavalrymen, so that the fort's power was confined to local control.

Malcom had lost twenty pounds and his face was drawn, his cheek-bones prominent. He was pale under his natural tan, and his hands shook a little as he pulled on his clothing. He winced, grimacing as pain shot through his left side, a reminder that his wound was not yet healed. A bandage was firmly fastened across his back, where that bullet had driven. An army surgeon had probed for and removed the slug and because of Malcom's youth and clean living habits he had begun to recover in spite of what had seemed irreparable damage. He was not yet well, but was mending fast; and he was too restless to stay in bed longer.

An orderly came in and saw him pulling on his shirt.

"Hey, get back in bed!" he ordered.

Malcom shook his head. "I ain't stayin' here no longer, soldier. I got work to do."

The orderly shrugged, and went out. When he returned with the surgeon, a blue-uniformed lieutenant with a cigar clipped in his bearded lips, Malcom was fully dressed. Following the doctor came the somber Wyatt Earp who had fetched Malcom to the fort on his load of buffalo hides. That jolting ride that had been a nightmare of pain and fainting spells, flavored with the odor of hides and cured meat.

"Take it easy," the surgeon commanded Malcom, frowning. "You've had a narrow squeak, my boy. Another week in bed'll be the best thing for you."

But again Herb Malcom shook his head. "I can't stay any longer, Lieutenant." Sadness was in his serious brown eyes, mingled with a determination which Wyatt Earp understood. "I got business to tend to."

The doctor gave him a quick examination, listening to the beat of the powerful Texan's heart.

"Steady enough," he reluctantly admitted. "But you're taking a big chance, moving. I warn you."

"Thanks, Lieutenant. But I got to take it." The youth's straight lips were drawn in a line of grim unhappiness.

Wyatt Earp was Malcom's age, but he had been around and on his own for many more years than had the young Texan from Rose Valley. Through the Civil War, Malcom had stayed home, a dutiful son taking care of the ranch while his father fought and died for the South. The lean, handsome Earp understood what bothered Malcom, for he had not only listened to the young fellow's delirious ravings, ravings about the ruin of Rose Valley, and of the Texans who had trusted him with the herd, but of Betsy White.

Earp made no attempt to dissuade Malcom, for he was a fierce individualist, as were most frontiersmen, believing a man had the right to live or die as he chose. Nor could anything the surgeon say change Malcom's determination.

"I need a hoss and then I'll be ridin'," Malcom declared.

The doctor shook his head. "Then take it easy as you can, sir, till that hole in you fully heals," he advised. "Don't blame me if it opens again."

Malcolm thanked him gratefully. Earp had spare horses, and suggested:

"S'pose we head for Abilene together, Malcom? I sent my hides on and I got business there."

Malcom nodded. "I reckon that's where Loman and Donnolly and them Indians took our cows, don't you?"

"Yeah, as far as Pryor and me could judge. But yuh'll never get 'em back, Herb, not now, unless the Rio Kid has already managed it. They run that herd full speed for the pens and they'll ship 'em pronto. Bet they're already on their way to market, and that the rustlers have pocketed the cash."

"Think we'll find the Rio Kid in Abilene?" asked Malcom.

"Mebee. We'll try, anyways," Wyatt Earp replied.

It took them a day to make the City of the Plains. It was Malcom's first look at a big market town and the bustle and excitement kept his eyes busy and his tongue silent. They crossed Mud Creek, and hit across the railroad through Texas Abilene. Leaving the horses at a livery stable, Malcom trailed Wyatt Earp to the Alamo Saloon.

A big man, as tall as Earp, with a flowing mustache, and wearing ivory-handled cap-and-ball Colts, got up from a table and strolled to meet them.

"Howdy, Wyatt!" he greeted cordially.

"Hello Bill! Want yuh to meet a friend of mine — Herb Malcom. This is Wild Bill Hickok, Herb."

Malcom was aware of the sharp scrutiny of the Marshal of Abiline.

"Texas man?" demanded Hickok.

"Yeah, but he's all right," Earp told the marshal. "He's had a streak of powerful bad luck, Bill. Rustlers workin' in cahoots with Virgil Colorado's renegades massacred a couple dozen of his friends on the Trail and stole several thousand longhorns. Malcom here was trail boss and he's huntin' a feller named Dog Donnolly and a friend of Dog's named Tank Loman."

"Huh!" growled Hickok, frowning. "Then yuh must be a friend of that young galoot they call the Rio Kid?"

"Shore am!" exclaimed Malcom. "Have yuh seen him, Marshal?"

"Have I seen him!" Hickok rapped on the bar for drinks. "They're on me, boys." He laughed a little. "I shore did see the Kid. He turned the town on its head the other night. Yuh'll have to visit Boot Hill if yuh wish to see what's left of Dog Donnolly. The Kid shot him at Ben Thompson's Bull's Head. There was a riot and I had to do my duty and arrest Pryor."

"Then yuh've got his locked up?" asked Earp. "Why, he's all right, Bill. There's no doubt Donnolly was in with them cow thieves."

"Loman, too?"

"Donnolly and Loman traveled together," declared Malcom. "Is Loman in town?"

Wild Bill hesitated before replying. "He was," he said at last. "But I don't want any promis'cous gunnin' in the streets, Malcom. I'll arrest him if yuh got any charges. Any evidence?"

Malcom shrugged. "I know Loman's in on it, Marshal. If we find the cows —"

"Yeah, if yuh find 'em. Well, I ain't seen Loman the past couple days, not the Rio Kid either. He escaped."

Wyatt Earp looked sharply at Wild Bill. The lean frontiersman's wide mouth turned up at the corners and his eyes lighted. He knew that Hickok had let his prisoner go.

"C'mon, Malcom, yuh look hungry," Earp invited. "I'm sorta empty myself. Let's go

189

next door and fill up."

Wild Bill nodded good-by, eyeing Herb Malcom calculatingly.

"Remember what I told yuh, boy," he said slowly. "Yuh can hunt yore cows but I don't want no shootin' 'less'n yuh're attacked. I'll do the shootin' if it's necessary."

Earp led Malcom outside. "Bill's a good man," he said. "He keeps order in this town, and that's a man's job. He has a lot of trouble with wild hombres off the Texas Trail."

Malcom said nothing. Only the small, set lines about his lips told Earp what would occur if he came up with his enemy.

"Wyatt," he said suddenly, then, "I'll never go home agin 'less I find them steers or make Loman pay. The folks depended on me, and I've failed 'em."

" 'Twasn't yore fault," insisted Earp.

"Mebbe not, but jest the same I've been beat. The folks back home are watchin' for us, expectin' us to fetch home the money they need so bad. And it's more'n jest that they're pore and need help. They borrowed money and put up their Valley holdin's to send that herd up the Trail. Now they won't be able to pay, and everybody'll lose everything, what little they got."

After eating, Malcom left Earp and wandered to the yards, starting to look over the many cattle there. He kept hoping to recognize some of the steers he had driven up the Chisholm Trail. Even should the brands have been switched he figured he could put his finger on individual steers from his long association with them. But though he kept on until dark, he came on nothing to help him in his search.

Going back uptown, he stood on the corner, watching the passersby — the buffalo hunters, bullwhackers, railroad builders, gamblers and dancehall girls. At last he walked over and sat down on a wooden bench facing the square. The lights of the city blazed high, and it was warming up for the night's fun. Raucous shouts, the shriller cries of women, the thudding of hoofs as cowboys rode in from the trail camps made up a din confusing to a range-bred lad like Malcom. Still, it was exciting, and for a time he forgot his misery, his own failure, for he blamed himself entirely for the ruined hopes of Rose Valley.

Three Conestoga wagons, with prairie schooner canvas tops, came creaking from a side street and headed south. The drivers wielded their lashes expertly, cursing and whipping at the six-horse teams. They caught Malcom's wandering eye but it was not until he saw the cavalcade that rode a short distance in the rear of the covered wagons that he leaped to his feet, the thrill of desperate hope in his quickening heart.

There were a couple of dozen riders in the band. Well mounted, they had rifles in saddle slings. The lamplight caught the burnished equipment of their small-arms, pistols in cartridge belts, the hilts of long knives. Hard-faced, steel-eyed fighting men they were.

"Why, that — that red-haired devil, I saw him with Loman!" gasped Herb Malcom.

On the outside of the unevenly spaced group rode a gunman lieutenant. Malcom remembered the horse, and the man too. He had seen them during the skirmish when the Rio Kid had led the Texans to save Wyatt Earp near the Red River.

Malcom hustled across the street, narrowly missing being run down by some hard-riding cowboys who were whooping it up on their way in. He ran along the edge of the road, eyes fixed on the wagons and the horsemen behind them. The cavalcade turned to the left, across the main thoroughfare, and cut up a side alley.

Malcom crossed after them, eagerly trailing the red-headed gunman he had recognized as one of Tank Loman's cronies. He paused at the entry to the alleyway, and saw that the three Conestoga wagons were being backed up to the loading patform of a large warehouse which ran through to Railroad Street.

The doors were opened wide. A lantern gave light to the loaders, as wooden boxes were fetched from the interior and placed in the big wagons. They were of various shapes. Some that were several feet long seemed unusually heavy, for it took two men to handle them. Others were square, made of thick boards. There were barrels, too.

Engrossed in watching, Herb Malcom suddenly realized that a horseman was swinging into the alley toward the warehouse. He looked up and saw Tank Loman himself.

The recognition was mutual. Loman's evil eyes lit with a startled, fearful hatred.

"Why, damn yuh!" he shouted, and his hand fell to the pistol at his broad waist, for he knew only too well how dangerous a witness the Texan would prove against him.

The surprise of the meeting caught Malcom off guard. His hand sought his Colt, but his belt had slipped around, for he was not a trained gunfighter. Loman had him!

A twisted grin showed the yellowed, gritted teeth of the killer, as Loman's pistol rose to drive a death slug through Malcom. But an instant before Loman fired, pointblank — he could never have missed Malcom's head — the mustang under the big gunny suddenly snorted and leaped high into the air. The murderous horseman's Colt banged, flashed fire, but the slug rapped into the side of the building over Malcom's Stetson.

The cursing Loman sought to fight down his maddened horse's head but the beast shot forward toward the wagons.

A slim, dark figure in a high-peaked Mexican hat came into Malcom's startled range of vision as the horse passed him. A shaft of light glinted on the twelve-inch blade of the sheath knife gripped in the hand of Malcom's savior.

"Celestino!" cried Malcom.

"Queeck, run!" ordered young Mireles. "No time to spik!"

The lad's sharp face was set, shadowed by the tall hat. His curved lips were twisted, and his expressive eyes rolled in excitement. He had jabbed his hunting knife into the mustang's rump just as Loman had taken aim at Malcom.

They heard Tank Loman's cursing, bellowed orders as they dashed away.

"Boys — pronto! Hustle out and get 'em!"

Gunmen leaped on horses, to trail Malcom and Celestino. The Mexican lad and the young trail boss ran down the block and turned into an alleyway as Loman surged out on the street, followed by his gunnies.

"There they go!"

A bullet bit a chunk of wood from the corner of the building around which the two pursued had just swung. Celestino leaped around another corner as the enemy came full-tilt through the alley, one at a time due to the confined space.

The shots and uproar brought Wild Bill Hickok bounding from the Alamo, running toward the scene of commotion.

Malcom's breath came pantingly as he ran. His lung that had been injured by the bullet began sending shooting pains through his body, and spots danced before his eyes. His knees almost buckled under, and he staggered. Weakness was swiftly overtaking him.

"Come, come!" urged young Mireles, turning as Malcom lagged.

"Go — ahead —" panted Malcom. "I — I'll —"

He would have gone down had Celestino not seized him by the arm.

"Queeck — duck under here!"

The quick-witted Mexican youth had at

that instant seen the black opening under a building, where the earth fell away. Big rocks formed a foundation for the lower corners — an ideal hiding place!

CHAPTER XVII:
THE LOST FOUND

Pushing under the building, Malcom and Celestino Mireles lay on the cool dirt, panting, the musty odor strong in their widened nostrils. Herb Malcom could not stop the heaving of his tortured lungs. He held his bandanna to his mouth in an effort to muffle his breathing.

The legs of the gunnies' horses showed a few feet away as the two hidden beneath the building froze, pistols in hand, for a last fight.

"Sam," they heard Tank Loman say, cursing, "here comes that nosy marshal! Go back and hold him till we rout Malcom out."

"Right," the man called Sam growled, swinging his mustang and trotting back to the alley opening.

With their ears keened to every sound, the two under the building waited. Loman pushed on to the next turn in the alley, then came back.

"I don't see 'em," they heard him say to his men. "We better split up some, boys. Can't let that damn Texas fool loose in town to spoil our game."

"Mebbe they're hid somewheres," a gunny suggested, and at that moment from the passage which ran at right angles into the alleyway, came Wild Bill's strident, commanding voice.

"Drop yore guns and get offa that hoss, Riley! What's the idea — shootin' up my town? Where's Tank Loman? I want him for rustlin'."

"You go plumb to hell," Riley's heavy voice growled.

"Hear that, Tank?" a gunny said in a low tone. "Hickok's after yuh. Malcom must've hollered."

"Damn him, he won't holler long — and he can't prove nothin'," Loman snarled.

"Yuh better get outa town, though," came the advice. "Wild Bill's a bad hombre to fool with. We got business in the south anyhow. You gotta stay free. Jest leave things to me in town here."

"Reckon yuh're right, Baldy," Tank Loman said huskily. "I'll meet yuh on the Trail."

He rode rapidly away, putting distance between himself and Wild Bill. Out in the street, Wild Bill, ivory-handled guns still in their supple holsters, faced the mounted gunny, Sam Riley, his jaw stuck out, eyes narrowed.

"Git down, I say!" Hickok commanded, ominously quiet.

Riley shrugged. "All right. What the hell! I'll get down, Hickok, but yuh'll suffer for this, I promise yuh."

Riley rose in his saddle; but instead of dismounting beside Hickok he suddenly threw himself off the other side of his horse so that the mustang's thick body was between him and the marshal of Abilene.

Crouched in the dirt beside his horse, Riley's gun flashed up. The famous gunfighter, Wild Bill Hickok, made his own draw, famous as the swiftest and most deadly on the frontier. The marshal's ivory-handled Colt streaked into action with the speed of sleight-of-hand. The moving weapon and the hand gripping it were just a blur. A fraction of a second ahead of Riley, who had made his cunning play, but a play divined by the expert Hickok, Wild Bill fired close under the mustang's belly. Riley's pistol flared, too, but the slug just kicked up dirt between Hickok's spread boots.

Riley's notched revolver sagged in his grip, fell on top of the man's burly body as the gunny took the force of Hickok's lawful bullet through the heart. He was dead before he rolled to a stop in the dirt.

Hickok checked him before letting the ivory-handled Colt slide back into its holster. Then, with long strides, he walked down the alley, pausing to look up the side alley from which the mounted gunmen of Tank Loman had prudently taken their departure a minute before.

"Huh!" grunted Hickok.

The two hidden under the building heard him swearing under his breath, and Malcom shifted.

"Remember, say nothing of the wagons," breathed Celestino. "Ees the game of my general, the Rio Keed."

Malcom sang out to Hickok weakly and the marshal came slowly toward them, watching them crawl out from under the house.

"What the hell yuh doin', huntin' rats?" he demanded with a grin, as he recognized Malcom.

"Runnin' from 'em," Malcom replied. "That was Loman and his bunch, Marshal."

"Yeah, I jest shot Sam Riley, one of Tank's pals. He tried the old hoss trick on me but I've seen it too often to lose on it."

Curiously he stared at the slim, dark-faced

Celestino.

"Howdy, Mex," he said. "How'd you horn in on this business?"

"He's a friend of mine," said Malcom. "He helped drive steers up the Trail."

"Huh! Well, get on out and haid for bed somewheres, both of yuh. I'll keep an eye peeled for Loman. Ain't much I could do on yore rustlin' charge, but now I want him for disturbin' the peace and attempted murder."

"He's headed for the tall timber," Malcom replied.

On the lighted street, Mireles nodded to the trail boss.

"Senor, you go sleep," he advised. "I hav' beesness to mak'. In the mornin' pairhaps I see you."

The thin young Mexican slid off into the darkness. Malcom, worn out, found a bed in a livery stable and soon slept, exhausted by the events and by his own weakness.

In the morning, uncertain how to look for the information, he wandered through the street again. Cattle buyers, brokers and cowmen were busy at the yards, though the inhabitants of Abilene who made their livings at night in saloons and gaming halls were still asleep. The warehouse where he had come upon Tank Loman was closed; the wagons were gone. Nor did he see anything of young Celestino Mireles.

After the heat of the noon sun passed, Malcom started his restless lookout in Abilene. He kept hoping to come upon some new clue, or to again see Loman, but the life of the busy cattle metropolis went on about him, with no attention paid to the forlorn stranger from Texas. He felt alone, beaten.

"I'll never go back home again!" he swore. "I'll die first!"

He had the fierce, deep pride of the Southerner, a pride that would never let him admit such a defeat. The trail from Texas has taken hundreds of young men. Even without such reasons as Herb Malcom had, many of them never went back home. New ties, new chances to make money by hunting, fighting or developing the frontier, or perhaps a bullet from a gunman's Colt, kept them.

The folks back home waited, mothers and fathers and sweethearts, for the hoofbeats that meant their young men were returning. Sometimes they waited for a lifetime. That was what now faced Betsy White, Malcom's sweetheart. He would never go back a beaten man.

He was thinking of Betsy, trying to put

thoughts of her out of his pain-filled heart.

"She ain't for me," he muttered. "Not now."

And his grim eyes, stern with unhappiness, suddenly saw a vision. For he was sure it was a vision, when he turned and saw Betsy herself hurrying toward him.

But her voice was real — and filled with emotion.

"Herb — Herb, dear!"

A terrible weakness that he could not control shook him. She was real! And the sight of her was too much for him, still suffering as he was from his wound.

"Betsy — Betsy!" was all he could say, brokenly.

Then she was in his arms, kissing his lips, smiling into his eyes.

"Oh, I knew it, I knew it! I just knew you couldn't be dead, Herb! I made them come! I knew I'd find you."

The warm softness of her sent happiness thrilling through every nerve of the worn young trail boss.

Now he knew — knew that nothing made any difference as long as he had Betsy.

"How — why — where'd yuh come from?" he demanded, as he watched her smiling face, seeing only the joy in it, and unaware of how long it had been pale from the fearful strain and anguish over her sweetheart's fate. Her determination, strengthened by the love she had for Herb Malcom, had forced her on and now she had found him. Betsy White was one woman who would not pine away with a broken heart, staring into the vast distances for the return of her man.

"It was your horse made me come up the Chisholm Trail, Herb," she told him. "He came back home with a bullet crease in his hide. Your saddle was covered with dried blood. I knew something terrible must have happened."

"Yeah, Blackie would head for home!" Malcom said. "The Indians caught the rest of the folks on the drive, but I got loose."

"Malcom!" The young trail boss turned to see Colonel Amos White stumping toward him, hand outstretched. Behind Betsy's father were a dozen of the older men from Rose Valley, Civil War veterans and friends of Malcom and his folks. These were the people the trail herd had been supposed to save from a cruel poverty, to start afresh in a hard life.

Also with them was John Barrett, the bluff merchant from Piketown, Texas, who had staked the drive.

He was smiling in his hearty manner, the

sun wrinkles deep about his blue eyes.

"Howdy, Malcom," Barrett said, grabbing the young cowman's hand. "Yuh had trouble, I hear, on the Trail. I was headin' to Rose Valley on a little business when I met the colonel and his friends startin' after yuh. Figgered I'd come along, too. I'm powerful sorry yuh run into hot water."

"Mr. Barrett's been mighty decent Herb," Amos White said gravely. "Helped us ride the Trail here. And he says for us not to worry."

"That's right," Barrett declared heartily. "Don't let what yuh couldn't help worry yuh, boy!" He slapped young Malcom on the back, and grinned. "Colonel, did I tell yuh I'd oughta be thankin' yuh for lettin' me come north with yuh? I'm fixin' to do a right nice stroke of business. I'm goin' to arrange so's all my merchandise'll be sent south from the railroad. It'll save me money."

Herb Malcom actually hated to face them, feeling responsible as he did for all that had been lost. Betsy, though, was not caring about cows or money, now that she had found him. She kept hold of his arm as though she feared he might get away from her.

In terse sentences the trail boss repeated

for the benefit of the Texans his story of the massacre. Every man among them had lost some relative — a son or a nephew.

They took it silently, that cruel blow of bitter fate. Life, for them, had always been hard, and tragedy to be expected.

"No chance of gettin' back the steers?" Colonel White asked after that long poignant silence, breaking the pall of grief which had overwhelmed them.

Herb Malcom shook his head. "Loman's already sold the cows and left town," he said dully. "There ain't much evidence against him. If we could find him, though. . . . Well, I'd jest like to get my hands on him!" Malcom's powerful fingers clenched, and his mouth was grim.

Colonel Amos White turned to John Barrett with a sigh.

"Yuh hear, Barrett? That means we can't pay yuh for stakin' us. It'll take a couple of years to make up another trail herd. We picked the best we had for the run."

Barrett put a hand on the veteran's sleeve.

"Forget it, White," he said kindly. "You ain't thinkin' I'd be hard on yuh? With all yuh've gone through?"

The colonel sighed heavily. "Well, anyway, yuh've got our notes and mortgages. And we'll shore pay 'em, give us time."

"Yuh'll get all the time yuh want, Colonel," assured the storekeeper heartily. "What yuh worryin' for, anyhow? I ain't."

"Thanks, thanks," Colonel White said. "Yuh're mighty decent, Barrett."

Chapter XVIII:
The Rio Kid's Strategy

When the sober cavalcade of Rose Valley people pulled out of Abilene the next day, Barrett alone remained in town to finish up his business, promising to follow within a few days.

Herb Malcom trotted his horse beside Betsy White's gentled mare. His thoughts were bitter as he considered reality with the way he had once expected to be returning to Rose Valley.

"I shore made one awful mess of things," he mourned.

"Don't, Herb!" ordered Betsy. "You're alive. That's the big thing."

With their carbines in slings, and holstered pistols, most of them cap-and-ball affairs used in the Confederate Army, the veterans strung out, headed home. No one had much to say. They were thinking of the dead youths on the Trail, and about what they could do to pay off their debts and start again. Everything they could scrape up and borrow had gone into the big herd. Since that hope was destroyed it was hard to see hope anywhere else.

The first night out from Abilene they camped on the bank of a creek. They arose at dawn, ate a skimpy breakfast, and once more hit the southern road. Dull miles rolled behind them — it was ride, pause, ride; camp for the night.

Herb Malcom rode with Betsy at the rear of the procession. He was still weak from what he had gone through, and as they approached the narrow valley in which the horrible massacre had occurred his face went deadly white.

"That's where it happened, Betsy," he muttered.

He steeled himself for the ordeal of passing the place, but memory of the awful nightmare he had gone through returned in full force to weigh down his spirit. Again he could feel the anguish he had undergone.

Colonel White and Job Potter — who had lost two sons on the Trail — were at the head of the line as they went through the gap into the narrow depression. Once inside, still following the beaten Chisholm Trail, they rode under the hot sun until they saw the gleam of light on white skeletons ahead — dead horses that had been picked clean by coyotes and vultures.

And as they came abreast of the last camp of the Rose Valley trail drivers, Colonel White gave a sharp cry of warning, raised a hand toward the bush-covered slopes to the west.

"Indians!" he shouted. "Guns ready, men!"

A band of painted savages, mounted on long-haired mustangs, swept toward them, shouting and firing. Within seconds defense was organized. Texan guns banged and without hesitation they shot their horses, to form a ring of animal flesh as a breastwork. This was life or death.

Flat on the warm dirt behind the bodies of their mounts, they began shooting their carbines at the increasing flood of Indians. Good marksmen, they seldom missed a target and they wasted no bullets. Each volley from them sent the charging savages swerving to the flanks, riding a wild circle about them.

Betsy White lay close to her sweetheart, swiftly loading for Malcom — and she knew that he would save a bullet for her at the end.

Gunfire grew deafening, smoke puffs rising to join in a dense cloud over their head.

Herb Malcom, bobbing up over the round belly of his still-warm horse, aimed his carbine again and again, each time killing an enemy. But he knew they could never beat off such a horde, for hundreds of Indians were pouring in on them.

Two men in the little ring of defenders were already wounded. Then another man was hit in the head, dying instantly. Still, for an hour the Texans managed to hold the killers off, firing only when they must, for they had none too much ammunition.

"There's that big chief," Malcom growled suddenly, as he glimpsed the giant redskin who had been the Nemesis of Rose Valley.

He saw the painted, devilish savage who had raided the Rose Valley herd, who had led the attacks on the trail camps. Now the big man was urging the others to the kill — talking with the burly, low-browed half-breed, Virgil Colorado. And it would not be long now for the little band of Rose Valley pioneers. They could not much longer hold out against the hellish attack. . . .

Bob Pryor, the Rio Kid, rode his dun horse Saber beside a tall, handsome man on a spirited bay. Saber, jealous of the powerful army mount Dandy, whose little dancing trot carried his famous master mile after mile on grueling campaigns, bared his teeth and nipped at Dandy, who returned the compliment and tried to fight.

General George Armstrong Custer, the Rio Kid's former commander in the Union Army, whom the Kid had ridden for through the years of conflict and followed into great battles in cavalry charges, grinned and spoke softly to Dandy. He was very fond of animals.

"That dun of yours is a rascal, Captain," he remarked. "Always was. However, he's about the fastest thing on four legs I've ever seen."

Custer, the great "Boy General," was just coming into his own as the country's Number One Indian fighter. After the war he had marched through Texas, where he had demonstrated against the invaders of Mexico and incidentally assisted the Rio Kid in smashing carpetbaggers who had been preying on the Rio Kid's homeland.

On campaign, in the wilds, Custer wore fringed buckskins and a broad hat. He had a tawny mustache, a strong chin, and fine eyes that could pierce a man, read him in an instant. Bob Pryor loved Custer and admired him. The affection was returned by the general.

Custer had just brought his regiment back from the Washita where a long campaign against Indian raiders had proved successful.

They were weaving through bushy land, high and rocky, toward the east.

"There's the Chisholm Trail, General," the Kid said.

Pryor was scouting ahead for the regiment, and Custer had chosen to ride with him. Danger was what both men lived on, and they knew each other well, knew that each could be depended upon to the last. Under Custer's long leg rode a Spencer carbine; he carried Colts and a hunting knife. This was "Pahuska," or "Long Hair," the man the Indians had come to respect as a terrific fighting man, yet a fair dealer.

"They don't understand the Indian back East," the general went on, resuming the subject of which they had been speaking. "The only way to fight them is to surprise them and hit them hard, Captain. They will not stand against troops. Our army horses, the general run of 'em, can't hope to catch the fast Indian mustangs. You must be bold, for you can't wait to bring up artillery and get into formal battle array. Else the Indians will simply leap on their ponies and leave you holding an empty sack."

The Rio Kid, after having left Abilene on Wild Bill Hickok's tip, had come upon

Custer in camp to the west. The general was hunting for raiding Indians, because complaints had come in that herds on the trails had been attacked, that outlying settlers' cabins had been burned, and the occupants killed or taken as slaves by the marauders.

"If we can catch the men who are supplying them with guns and ammunition," Custer told the Kid, "it will be a feather in my cap. I believe Virgil Colorado's behind these new outbreaks, though there is no telling who is back of him. Somebody who can afford to spend money — for the young braves shot in the fighting have carried new Spencer carbines and rim-fire cartridges. It makes them much more dangerous when they have modern weapons."

The Kid's information concerning Tank Loman's connection with Colorado, his story of the massacre on the Chisholm Trail, and his assurance that he could lead the cavalry to trap the gun-runners, had caused Custer to march promptly. Whoever was supplying the savages with deadly weapons must be run to earth.

The long column of the regiment strung out behind the leaders, the Rio Kid and General Custer. Officers rode the flanks. The troopers in their blue uniforms and felt hats were armed with carbines and sabers, and guidon carriers with each troop made a martial picture. And in the rear of the column came the supply wagons, blue-bodied, canvas-topped affairs carrying food, ammunition, equipment.

"It's Loman's gang that's supplying Colorado's renegades," repeated Bob Pryor, as he and General Custer rode along. "I'm sure of that, from what I've seen and heard myself, but I don't know who is back of Loman — if anybody. I do know, though, that they've planned to hit the herds on the trail from Texas — mean to make a regular business of it, General."

"The Trail must be kept clear," Custer agreed. "That's obvious. This cattle raising looks as though it would prove to be a great industry. The East needs beef; the West needs a market; the South must have money for reconstruction. It's up to the army to protect the drivers. This is wonderful country, Pryor."

The general's eyes gazed out over the vast land, foreseeing the future, foretelling it.

"One day," he mused prophetically, "millions of people will live here, mark my words. It may not seem possible now, but it'll come. Why, the railroads are building thousands of miles of track through the States and even into the territories where they said a few years back that no white man could set foot. The iron rails are being projected every which way — east and west, north and south. There's one planned to reach even to Texas, to carry cattle northward and goods back south."

Pryor nodded. "They won't need any Chisholm Trail," he remarked, "once they finish the railroad, General."

"No, they won't. . . . Look out, someone's riding toward us!"

The two, out in advance of the cavalry regiment, drew aside into the bush, waiting for the horseman coming toward them. Their expert eyes had noted the slight sign that betrayed the riders presence — a tiny flash of the sun on metal accoutrements.

Then a slim figure on a black horse came into their range of vision. He was riding cautiously, his black eyes roving from left to right. Before reaching the spot where they waited, he drew up, staring at a disturbed leaf which Saber's rump had brushed when the Kid had shoved him quickly into hiding.

Plainly the wary horseman believed a trap had been laid for him.

Then the Rio Kid gave a low whistle, and shoved Saber out into the trail.

"Celestino! So yuh did get here!"

Young Mireles' dark eyes lighted as he recognized his friend.

"General," he cried. "At las' you come!"

General Custer, following the Kid on Dandy, nodded to Pryor's young Mexican friend. They had met on the Border two years before, when Custer had ridden the Rio Grande line.

"Any luck?" Pryor asked Celestino, in a low voice.

He had gambled heavily on Celestino's ability as a spy. Failure to locate Colorado's killers, and to catch Loman red-handed, would mean that Custer would be on a wild-goose chase, on the Rio Kid's say-so. To come up with roving Indian bands in the vast Nations was like hunting a needle in a haystack.

"*Si, si,* General," whispered Celestino. "You weesh me to talk now, before the great soldier? You mus' hurry, I tell you."

The Kid read the youth's repressed excitement. The dark Mexican eyes flashed with spirit.

"Go to it — let's have it all," ordered the Rio Kid, and promptly Celestino began to tell his story.

"Las' night," he reported, "after trailing three large wagons, General, wheech thees Tank Loman owns, finally I come upon zem. Ees Virgil Colorado — I hear zem say hees name, for I am lie in bush close to camp. Loman geeve zem hundreds of new rifle', bullets by thousan'. Also many barrel' of whiskey, wheech zey dreenck so I am able to get ver-ee close up. Zose Indian' go wild weeth likker, *si*. Was dark, zey hav' fire an' powwow. Loman say, 'Now we heet ze Trail, Virgil. Tak' all Texas cows we want. Plenty mon-ee, plenty guns.'"

The daring young Mexican had lain in the thick bush, in a cramped position, four hours, his ears and eyes keenly busy. The Indians had grown maudlin, and so had Tank Loman and his gunnies. Before light came, Celestino had started his cautious retreat, knowing he must escape before some Indian smelled him out in the daylight.

"Zen, from a heeltop, General," the lad reported, repressed excitement in his voice, "as dawn she came, I see zat beeg Indian chief, same one who attack us on ze Trail. He come, he keek Loman awake. Many braves tak' zeir new guns and bullets and ride south for ze Trail. I hide, to sleep, for I mus' be ready when you come."

"That means the big chief must have led them out on a raid," General Custer said quickly. "That's several hours ago, and there's no telling where they went. It's too bad we couldn't have caught Loman with Colorado, in camp with his wagons and guns."

"Loman deed not ride weeth zem," Celestino explained. "He drank too much. He stay weeth some Indians in camp. Ees not far from here."

"Take us there," ordered Custer. "Pryor, ride ahead and scout the way. I'll go back and pick out detachments that we can use for the attack."

He swung Dandy and galloped back toward his regiment.

Chapter XIX:
Battle

Celestino Mireles pointed the way for the Rio Kid. East for a mile, then cutting south along a narrow deer trail.

Pryor left markers for Custer to follow him by.

"Quiet, now," whispered Celestino, when they had ridden an hour through the winding path. "Eef zey are steel zere, eet ees on ze nex' bend of zat creek."

Dismounting then, the two crept forward, and the Rio Kid peered through interstices of chaparral at the scene, which was as Celestino had described it. It was a temporary camp. Indian braves lounged about, sleeping off the effects of Tank Loman's whiskey. The three wagons which had brought the contraband arms and liquor to the savages stood at the edge of the natural clearing on the stream's bank.

Tank Loman was standing in the shade of a huge live-oak, staring south toward the

Chisholm Trail.

"I want him," Pryor muttered tightly.

There were about a hundred Indians, young fighters, in the camp. The rest had evidently ridden out with Virgil Colorado and the tall chief who had given the alarm.

Indian mustangs were close at hand, ready for use. After a time, the Kid whispered:

"Yuh hear that? It's what Loman's listenin' to, Celestino."

"*Si, si.* Ees mucho shooting below."

Dimly, cut off by the sharp ridge which flanked the southwest side of the Indian camp, could be heard the far-off explosions of guns.

"That must be where they went, to attack a party on the Trail," said the Kid, his eyes flashing angry fire.

He slipped back, to connect with Custer's advance. The general came out in front of his men when he saw Bob Pryor, who quickly reported to him.

Custer's method of fighting Indians was the approved way. He split his forces into three sections, under the command of subordinates, reserving one troop for himself. One group of troopers would circle around, to get to the south side of the camp; others would come in from the west, while Custer's immediate fighting men would

221

form a skirmish line and hit the north, driving the foe into the guns of the waiting troops.

He followed this course now in attacking the camp the Rio Kid had located. Allowing his men time to take their positions he drew his saber and, guidons waving in the breeze, the cavalrymen burst from their screen of bushes onto the Indian encampment.

Cries of alarm sounded. The naked, painted warriors leaped up, shooting as they fled to their mustangs, seeking to escape. Splashing across the creek as the troopers' pistols picked them off, they found themselves face to face with the general's other companies. Surrounded, the braves fought to the death or threw down their weapons, sullenly surrendering.

The Rio Kid, leaving the redskins to the troopers, kept an eye on Tank Loman's huge figure. Loman, hearing the notes of the bugle that ordered the cavalry charge, scuttled toward his horse, and tried to ride off eastward into the bush. But Bob Pryor, pushing Saber at full-tilt, the wind madly whistling past his ears, tugging at his strapped felt hat, fired a shot that sang within an inch of Loman's ear. The big fellow's eyes, as he turned to see who was after him so hotly, were red with sudden fright as he recognized the Rio Kid.

Swiftly he shot back at Pryor, but the pace of his horse on the uneven ground spoiled his aim. The Kid, teeth showing in a grin of triumph, whirled upon him as the swift dun overtook Loman's slower animal.

"Drop that gun or I'll drill yuh, Loman," shouted the Kid.

"Go to hell, damn yuh!"

Loman sought to take aim at Pryor. The Kid had to shoot, and shoot fast, for he was only five yards from his enemy. He let go with his revolver, and his shot hit, broke Loman's forearm. The big gunny dropped his Colt with a scream of anguish.

Then the Kid swept up to him and grasped the bridle of Loman's horse. The mustang sought to jerk away, eyes rolling madly, but Saber bit a mouthful of hair and hide out of him, lashing into the barrel ribs with a sharp hoof. Bullied, the animal stopped fighting and stood trembling as the Kid yanked Loman from his leather and quickly disarmed him of all weapons.

"Yuh're mine, Loman," growled Pryor, eying his captive. "And damn yuh, yuh're goin' to get some of what yuh've been givin' to others!"

His hard fist drove into Tank Loman's sharp-bridged nose, and blood spurted from

223

the blow. Loman dropped to one knee, flinging up his uninjured arm to shield his face.

"Stop it, Kid!" he howled.

As Pryor took a step toward him, nostrils flared, Loman began to whimper, begging for mercy.

"I was right," the Kid thought. "He's yeller enough to crack, damn him."

The firing was dying off to scattered shots, for the troopers had taken the majority of the Indians in the first charge. Custer was in the thick of it, using saber and pistol, urging his men on.

"Quick now!" said the Kid's steely voice, as his eyes drilled Loman. "Where's Colorado gone, Loman? What's that shootin' on the Trail?"

A glance at the fist of the Rio Kid started Loman talking. The Kid had read him right. Loman was tough only when he was winning.

"They — they're killing off them Rose Valley people," whined Tank Loman. "There's a big bunch of Injuns down there —"

With a curse, the Rio Kid swung, leaped to his saddle. He signaled a nearby trooper.

"Watch this man!" he snapped. "He's ringleader of the gun-runners. The general'll want him."

The trooper caught the military snap of

the order, and automatically saluted.

"Yes, suh," he replied.

General Custer was near the creek, over-seeing the prisoners that were being brought in. He heard the Rio Kid's report, and swiftly called orders to his officers.

Five minutes later, leaving guards on the prisoners at the camp, the body of Custer's cavalrymen were headed south for the Chisholm Trail.

"We should have men at the south end," said Custer, as the Rio Kid swiftly described the narrow valley of death. "And more on the ridges. However, there's no time for that now."

The grim-faced Rio Kid rode full-tilt for the gap entrance. Only the general's charger, Dandy, had been able to keep up with Saber, until now. Frontal attack suited Pryor, not knowing the meaning of fear.

He had learned from Tank Loman of the arrival in Abilene of Colonel Amos White and the other Rose Valley folks, and of the attack that had been plotted against the band of Texans — the attack that was now taking place.

His main idea was to save them from death.

He spurred Saber through the narrow gap at the north end of the valley, and out onto the flat of the plain where the terrific fight was going on. Ahead lay the circle of dead horses, with the beleaguered Rose Valley men behind them, down flat, using their final bullets on the Indian hordes that were ringing them.

Hundreds of Indians swarmed in the valley, their savage, painted faces grimacing the excitement of battle. They saw the Rio Kid enter the valley and pound toward them, his pistols roaring death. On the south flank of the savage band Pryor, through drifting dust and powder smoke, glimpsed the big Indian chief who had so persistently trailed and attacked the Rose Valley men.

Whirling redskins swung out of line and started at the Kid, attacking single-handed. Then Custer appeared, in his fringed buckskins, his long hair flying back from his handsome head under the strapped broad hat.

"Pahuska! Pahuska!" The cry rose shrill from many throats.

On the west slope Virgil Colorado sat a hairy, chunky mustang with rose-colored spots on his snow-white flanks. The renegade halfbreed who had plotted death and destruction to the trail drivers, whose cunning had armed his braves with new rifles and fed their vanity and fighting spirit, saw the person he feared — General George Custer, Pahuska. The Kid saw Colorado suddenly pivot his paint horse and cut west into the bush.

Now the troopers were coming through the gap, speeding to the attack, with guidons flying, and bugles sounding the attack, the clear notes echoing back from the hills. The firing rose to a terrific volume as the trained soldiers began shooting from their saddles, bearing down in the charge on the enemy.

The formation of the circle about the beleaguered Texans broke. Savages rode off in all directions, headed for the tall timber. They would not stand against trained troops.

As the lines of troopers swirled in, smoke and dust clouded the warm air of the wilderness. Curses and shots made a wild melee of sound.

The savages who had been rushing at the Rio Kid whirled their horses, retreating as they saw Custer and his troopers coming. Hundreds interposed between the Rio Kid and the south gap, where last he had seen the still unknown big chief who so hated them that he had followed them up from Texas.

"The General will want Colorado — but I

want Loman and that other killer," the Kid thought tightly, as his guns banged in his steady hand.

He swerved Saber, heading for the spot where he had last glimpsed the breed medicine man. Colorado was running for it westward, up the long slope toward the ridges. The paint pony made an easy mark for the Kid to follow, and he fought off other Indians who got in his way.

Troopers were following him, on the savages' trail. Back in the valley the swift movements of Custer's brigade had encircled a couple of hundred of the enemy.

Saber galloped at breakneck speed on the trail of Colorado's paint horse. Overtaking two braves who made an effort to stop him, the Kid sent a slug through one, and the other crashed headlong from his horse. Bob Pryor swept on.

The paint horse was climbing the steep slope when Saber came within pistol shot. Pryor fired, Saber steadying for him as he was trained to do. Colorado, low on the paint horse's bare back, turned, and the dark, sullen face grew blacker as he recognized the approaching Rio Kid. The medicine man fired a shot that cut a hole in Pryor's Stetson and clipped his hair. But at the Kid's second shot, Colorado slid off his paint horse's back and fell on his face in the grass.

Gun ready, the Rio Kid eagerly pressed forward. As he approached, however, the medicine man, playing 'possum, rolled over, prepared to fire pointblank into the Kid's body.

With a mighty bound, Saber reared, forehoofs cracking down hard on Virgil Colorado's body. A sharp hoof struck the breed's skull, and it cracked open like an eggshell hit by a hammer. Colorado's last slug grooved Saber's ribs and lodged in the cantle of the Kid's saddle.

Pryor slung the corpse on the paint horse, looped the arms in the rope halter, and started back to the valley.

Sporadic fighting still went on, but the troopers had won the swift battle. In the center of the valley General Custer sat Dandy, the blood of the fight on his face and clothing.

And here were the Texans of Rose Valley. Colonel Amos White was looking up into the general's strong face, thanking him for having saved them.

Betsy White was held in Herbert Malcom's arms. Seven others had survived the ordeal, having held out behind their ring of dead mounts until help had come. Some lay dead, in the circle. There was none who did not have a wound.

"Brought yuh Virgil Colorado, General," the Rio Kid reported.

"Good work, Captain," Custer exclaimed, looking over the dead medicine man. "That's one Indian we've reformed."

Swiftly the Kid hunted the battlefield for the body of the giant chief he sought. But he did not find the remains of his enemy. Custer told him that many redskins had escaped by way of the south gap.

"I'll make a trade with yuh, General," the Kid said, with a smile. "Yuh can have Colorado's body, but I want Tank Loman."

"He's the man who fetched in those guns, isn't he?"

"Yeah, but there's somebody behind him. I figger if I'm alone with Loman awhile, he'll agree to tell me all I wanta know."

Custer shrugged.

"You've done fine work, Captain. I could hardly refuse you such a favor. I'll deputize you as a scout on special army duty. Loman's yours."

Chapter XX:
The Hills Are Red

The meeting of Rose Valley pioneers, held on the wide veranda of Colonel Amos White's ranchhouse a few days later, was a sad affair. Most of these people mourned sons and friends lost on the Chisholm Trail. There was deep discouragement because their attempt to battle a tragic Fate had brought only terrible calamity.

Now the end of the world seemed to have come as a further crushing blow struck them. They loved Rose Valley, for it had become home to them — and they were to lose it!

John Barrett, the man who had staked them so they might make the big drive to Abilene, had come from Piketown. The big merchant, smiling, had shown Amos White the notes signed by the colonel and the other men of the valley, borrowing money with which to pay for supplies to stake them on the drive. These notes were due, and with them accompanying mortgages on the land claimed by the valley inhabitants.

White had called his friends together. They had come, bringing their families, and now anxious-eyed women with their children waited near at hand, sensing trouble.

A large party of men had ridden to the valley with John Barrett — steel-eyed fellows, armed with the usual complement of guns habitual to riders in the wilderness. They lounged in the shade of the big live-oaks in the colonel's yard.

"John Barrett," Colonel White told his friends gravely, "wants to say a word to us, friends."

The wooden-legged chief of the valley mopped sweat from his brow and wearily took a chair, head drooped. Betsy was sitting beside Herb Malcom, who was frowning.

John Barrett rose. "Folks," he drawled, "there's no use to look so sad. I told yuh not to worry, and yuh needn't. I'll take care of yuh. But I want the valley and you can't pay yore debts. Still, what's land in this country? I've arranged for yuh to move west, across the Pecos, to new soil."

"Can't we stay here, where we're home?" growled a man.

Barrett's smile disappeared. A harsh note

came into his voice.

"No, yuh can't!" he snapped. "The valley's mine, and I'm claimin' it, savvy?"

"Look — here comes the Rio Kid!" whispered Betsy to Herb Malcom.

Down the road came Bob Pryor. Two men were with him. Malcom suddenly leaped to his feet.

"Why, that's Tank Loman!" he cried.

Tank Loman rode with head down, one arm in a sling, the picture of dejection. As he looked up, fear came to his eyes. Angry men were starting for him as Bob Pryor pushed up to the porch of White's home and slid off the dust-covered Saber. Behind them rode Celestino Mireles, the slim Mexican lad.

All three showed signs of the hard, swift ride from Custer's bivouac in the Territory. Loman had several half-healed bruises on his sullen, ugly face, and there was a yellow look around his mouth.

Pryor left Tank to Celestino, as he bounded up the steps to face John Barrett.

"Here I am, Barrett!" he said, his voice ringing clear. "Come to pay off yore notes that yuh got from the Rose Valley folks. They run to three thousand dollars, and I got it in cash."

Scowling, his face reddening, Barrett

stared at Pryor. The clop of hoofs from the north road made him turn around. Half a dozen men were approaching.

"All right," he said rapidly. "Here yuh are, Pryor. Gimme the cash — I'll be ridin'."

Quickly the Kid made the payment and slung the signed papers to Herb Malcom. Barrett turned, but the Rio Kid seized his sleeve.

"Jest a minute, Barrett! Listen to what I say."

"To hell with yuh," Barrett growled.

But he froze as he saw the look in the Kid's eyes, saw him draw back a step, facing the gathering.

"Folks," Pryor began, "I know yuh look on Tank Loman as an enemy — and so he was till he got converted. He's told me what's behind yore troubles, behind the raids and murders in yore valley, and jest why our drive up the Trail turned into such a horrible massacre. For it wasn't chance that Virgil Colorado hit us the way he did. Look!"

The Rio Kid waved his hand toward the hills flanking Rose Valley. The sun, dropping in the west, turned them red as blood, and a ruby gleam came from the rocks and soil.

"Reason they're red," the Kid said slowly, clearly, "is that they're hills of iron ore, powerful rich stuff that's worth a big fortune, what with all these railroads buildin'. That's what Barrett's been after. You-all have got them hills claimed and he coveted 'em, so he started to get 'em by fair means or foul. He raided yuh to scare yuh out, but that didn't work so good. Then he saw his chance when yuh asked him for credit, and he had yuh sign away yore valley so's yuh could get the cattle herd to market. Through Loman and Dog Donnolly, he connected with Virgil Colorado. Loman and Donnolly had already planned to raid the Trail with Colorado and his Indians. Barrett follered the herd all the way up — and he rode disguised as an Indian chief, the big devil we spotted several times. H'es a murderer and robber! And the U. S. Army wants him for sellin' guns and likker to the Indians!"

"Yuh lie!" snarled Barrett, backed against the porch rail. "Yuh can't prove yore words, Pryor!"

"I got Tank Loman here, and I reckon yore disguise is hid in yore saddle-packs, Barrett. You knew the value of these ruby hills, and yuh knew that in a short time they'll build a railroad that'll hit within a few miles of Rose Valley, so yuh woulda stood to clean up millions. The first day I come through here, yuh killed two of the valley men who came on yuh prospectin' in the hills — shot 'em dead, Loman says, for fear they'd get suspicious as to the iron deposits. Now yuh're through, and under arrest!"

"By whose authority?" snapped Barrett, eyeing the Kid.

"I'm deputized by General George A. Custer to take yuh back for trial," Pryor said icily. "Unbuckle yore gunbelt and —"

"Never," shrieked Barrett, his face beet-red as fury frothed his lips.

A lifted hand brought his gunmen running toward the porch, pistols ready. Barrett dropped his right hand to his Colt revolver butt, making a swift draw.

The Kid's Colt flashed in the afternoon sunlight. Barrett fired too hurriedly, hoping to beat the steady, cool Rio Kid. The killer's bullet bit a chunk of leather from the Kid's boot toe. Barrett stood a second, arm dropping from his weapon's weight. A blue hole showed between his eyes. He teetered, then fell dead at Bob Pryor's feet.

Gun shots spat in the warm air of Rose Valley. The Texans grabbed up their weapons to bet off the charging killers enlisted by John Barrett. Bullets flew back and forth. Then the party of riders who had been approaching swept up. Accurate pistols banged as they galloped at Barrett's gang.

Wyatt Earp, Buffalo Bill, Bat Masterson, and half a dozen other buffalo hunters had come along to back up the play of their friend the Rio Kid. Before the awful blasting fire, the gunmen could not stand. Cursing, they turned and ran for their saddled horses in a vain hope of escape. Ruthlessly, the buffalo hunters ran them down. They shucked their weapons, crying for mercy.

Bob Pryor, the Rio Kid, stood over the body of the arch-foe of Rose Valley, John Barrett. A smile showed on his lips as his boyish face lighted with the realization of a job well done.

In the morning the Rio Kid was ready to head Saber northward for Kansas and Indian Territory. At hand was a led horse, and on the animal was the body of John Barrett.

"Reckon Custer'll be jest as glad to have him dead as alive," the Kid remarked to his tall friend, Wyatt Earp.

"Save him trouble," agreed Earp succinctly.

The folks of Rose Valley had collected to say good-by to the Rio Kid, the man who had saved them. Gratitude showed in their eyes, and Colonel Amos White shook his hand, thanking him and telling him he was

ever welcome in Rose Valley and that anything there was his.

"Yuh can sell off a couple of them hills of
iron," the Kid said, smiling, "and have
enough to live on forever, Colonel. *Adios,*
now."

He waved to Herb Malcom, standing with
Betsy at his side. New hope shone in the
trail boss' handsome face.

Buffalo Bill Cody started out in the van,
with Bat Masterson after him. A bunch of
hunters came next. They were going to drop
off in the Territory and complete their work.

Wyatt Earp rode at Bob Pryor's side.
Celestino Mireles, always looking for ways
to please his friend and mentor, the Rio
Kid, took the rope of the led horse and
dropped behind.

"What yuh goin' to do next, Kid?" Earp
inquired, as they left Rose Valley behind,
the Kid turning to wave a last good-by to
the people he had brought out of their
trouble.

"Dunno." The Rio Kid shrugged. "First,
I'll see Custer."

"Wild Bill Hickok told me to give yuh a
message, Kid. Said if yuh ever cleared yoreself so yuh could come back to Abilene, to
hunt him up. He'd like, he said, to have yuh
as a deppity marshal. And that goes for any

place he is."

The Rio Kid grinned.

"Might be sport at that, Wyatt. Reckon I'm clear now, with all this proved against Loman and Donnolly, and Barrett dead. I'll shore look Wild Bill up."

Ahead lay the Rio Kid's trail, the trail of a hard-fighting rider who would never cease to battle for the downtrodden, to buck evil no matter what the odds. History was being made on the frontier, and the Rio Kid was helping to make it right.